savage hearts

ANASTASI FAMILY SYNDICATE
BOOK 5

DORI PULITANO

Editor: Amy Briggs EditsByAmy.com
Cover Design: Taylored Designs
Author Dori Pulitano
www.AuthorDoriPulitano.com
This book has been re-edited to include new content.

family tree

Giuseppe Anastasi & Vittoria Anastasi
Grandfather/Deceased & Grandmother/live in Sicily

Giacomo Anastasi
Son to Giuseppe & Vittoria
Mafia Head in Sicily

Giorga Anastasi
Giacomo's Wife

Massimo Anastasi
Oldest son to Giacomo/Giorga/Mafia Head in Vegas/Owns
Discoteca Club

Madison Heart
Massimo's Fiancée

Vincenzo Anastasi
Second in Line/son to Giacomo/Giorga/Owns Bellissimo
Amore Restaurant

Riley Lawson
Vincenzo's Wife/Former FBI

Robert Deminico Anastasi & Veronica Gia Anastasi
Vincenzo & Riley's Twins

Antonio Anastasi
Third in Line/Son to Giacomo/Giorga/Owns Anastasi
Construction

Rachel Hill
Wife to Antonio &
Michael/Former Assistant
DA

Michael Brighton
Husband to Rachel &
Antonio/Anastasi Family
Attorney

Catarina Anastasi
Daughter to Giacomo/Giorga/Nurse

Donny Russo
Husband to Catarina/Massimo's Head Enforcer

Leonardo Enzo Anastasi
Catarina & Donny's Son

Celestina Anastasi
Daughter to Giacomo/Giorga/Carmela's Twin

Beckett Heart
Celestina's Love Interest

Emilia Beckett Heart
Daughter to Celestina & Beckett

Carmela Anastasi
Daughter to Giacomo/Giorga/Celestina's Twin/Clothing
Designer

notable characters

Alex Coulter
Former Detective/Head of Security at Discoteca (Massimo's Club)

Carlisle Casteneli
Former Detective/Head of Security at Discoteca (Massimo's Club)

Mike Donovan
District Attorney

Harley Cook
Catarina's Friend/Nurse/Drew's Wife

Drew Mancini
Enforcer/Harley's Husband

Miguel Angel
Sureños Leader/Alliance with Anastasi Family

Kevin Luchasi
Anastasi Family Doctor

Javier Costa
Gang Leader/Deceased

Manuel Costa
Javier's Brother/New Gang Leader

Matias Silva
Head of Chilean Mafia/Alliance with Anastasis

Cristian Silva
Chilean Mafia/Matias Brother/Alliance with Anastasis

Bastian Silva
Chilean Mafia/ Matias Brother /Alliance with Anastasis

Filippo Bianchi
Don to Italian Mafia (Rome)/Alliance with Anastasis

Lorenzo Bianchi
Son to Italian Mafia Don (Rome)/Alliance with Anastasis

series reading order

DANGEROUS ATTRACTION

MASSIMO & MADISON'S BOOK

DARK DESIRE

VINCENZO & RILEY'S BOOK

FATAL LOVE

ANTONIO, RACHEL & MICHAEL'S BOOK

DEADLY INTENTIONS

CATARINA & DONNY'S BOOK

CARNAGE HEART (NOVELLA)

BECKETT'S STORY

SAVAGE HEARTS

CELESTINA & BECKETT'S STORY

FRACTURED DEVOTION

CARMELLA & ALEX'S BOOK

Grab the entire series on E-Book at
https://alphabookboyfriends.com/collections/bundles/bundles

reader warning

Like most Mafia books, this one contains scenes that may be difficult for some to handle. Human trafficking, violence, and attempted suicide are all addressed in this book. If that is not something you can handle, please discontinue reading.

Suicide is a serious matter. If you or anyone you know in the United States is contemplating suicide, please seek help by reaching out to the Suicide & Crisis lifeline by dialing 988 from your phone. International assistance is available by clicking here.

Sometimes, we walk away from the love, thinking we're protecting the person we care about most, only to realize staying is exactly what both our hearts needed to stay whole.

DORI PULITANO

prologue

CELESTINA

ALL THREE OF my brothers stood like statues in the circular drive outside Vincenzo's house, their presence commanding and severe. Massimo's hands were buried in his pockets, his body taut as a coiled spring. Despite his seemingly relaxed posture, I could see the tension radiating off him like a palpable force. Vincenzo, always the enforcer, stood with his arms crossed over his broad chest, his glare cutting through the distance between us, filled with unspoken fury and concern. My gaze shifted to Antonio, the youngest, whose face betrayed a raw mixture of emotions—relief shadowed by worry, like he was holding his breath, afraid to let it out.

"Wait here." Tino's voice was sharp as he parked the car, the order laced with an edge that brooked no argument. He stepped out, leaving me alone with my jumbled thoughts and the sight of my brothers through the windshield. They seemed like a silent jury, and I couldn't read the verdict.

What happened next caught me off guard. Massimo, the stoic one, reached out and shook Tino's hand, his head nodding in what seemed like gratitude. My shock doubled when Vincenzo, all storm and steel, swept past them and wrenched open my door. His arms enveloped me in a bruising hug that knocked the breath from my lungs. He was holding me so tightly, as if I might disappear if he let go.

"Celestina." His voice was a rough whisper as he buried his face in my hair, his strong frame trembling against mine. "We thought we'd lost you." There was a desperate edge to his words, a confession of fear he'd never normally allow. He pulled back slightly, his hands firm on my arms as his eyes darted over me, searching for any sign of harm. When he saw the oversized shirt I was wearing, his gaze turned feral, a low growl rumbling in his chest. "Where the fuck are your clothes?"

"I don't have any. This is Beckett's shirt." I tore free of his grasp, my voice breaking as I pushed past him. "Where's Beckett?" I demanded, my eyes locking onto Massimo as I stepped in front of him, my heart hammering with a new, urgent fear.

"*Princessa*, I told you to forget about him." Tino's tone was softer now, almost pleading as he glanced at Massimo, a silent request for help.

Massimo's arm slid around my shoulders, pulling me close to his side, his warmth a stark contrast to the icy fear curling in my stomach. "Celestina let's go inside," he murmured in a soothing voice, but I could hear the strain beneath it. "Madison and the others are waiting for you. You need to rest, get cleaned up. We'll take care of everything else." His gaze shifted to Tino, a glint of steel in his eyes. "We'll be in touch about the agreement. Thank you for bringing our sister home."

Tino nodded, his expression unreadable as he got back into his car. "We'll definitely be in touch. I'm looking forward to our new business deal, Massimo." His words were calm, but there was something darker beneath them, a promise of things unsaid. He drove off, leaving a tense silence in his wake.

As soon as the car disappeared from sight, the fragile control I'd been clinging to shattered. A sob tore from my throat, my legs giving way beneath me. Massimo caught me effortlessly, his arms strong and secure as he lifted me.

He softly spoke, his voice a soothing remedy against the storm of emotions raging inside me. He carried me into the house, his steps sure and steady, while I crumbled in his arms.

The world blurred around me as I was laid gently on a soft mattress, familiar voices buzzing at the edge of my consciousness, but their words were lost in the torrent of my own sobs. I sensed a gentle hand on my shoulder providing stability, but all I could do was hold onto the material beneath me, my body quivering with every uneven breath.

I was dimly aware of voices around me, a chorus of concern that barely registered against the roar of my own grief. I sank onto the mattress, the familiar softness cradling me as if trying to soothe the turmoil inside. A gentle hand rested on my shoulder, grounding me, pulling me out of the darkness I was slipping into.

"What do you need, Celestina? Are you hurt? Should I have Catarina come check you over?" Massimo's voice, usually so steady and authoritative, now cracked with worry. The sight of his pained expression twisted the knife deeper into my chest.

"No," I whispered, my voice raw. I couldn't bear to look at him. His concern only made the ache worse. "There is nothing she can do to stop the pain."

Antonio, with his quiet strength, climbed onto the bed beside me and pulled me into his embrace. I pressed my face against his chest, feeling the steady beat of his heart, a cruel reminder of how shattered mine was. His arms around me were solid and safe, but they weren't the arms I wanted.

"What happened, Celestina?" His voice was a soft murmur against my hair.

"I fell in love with a man who doesn't want me," I choked out, the admission ripping through me like jagged glass. The tears came hot and fast, soaking into Antonio's shirt. I despised my own weakness, my vulnerability, but I couldn't stop. The words were a torrent, unstoppable. "He doesn't want me."

"Love?" Massimo's derisive snort sliced through the air. "Sweet girl, that man kidnapped you to hurt our family."

"I know that." I lifted my head, meeting his gaze with as much strength as I could muster. "But something changed. He went against Manuel Costa…for me." The memory of Beckett's defiance, the way he'd stood between me and danger, was a twisted, painful hope I clung to. "Where is he, Massimo? Where is Beckett?"

"It's not important." Massimo's pacing betrayed the struggle he was trying to hide. His hand raked through his hair, and he took a deep, shuddering breath. "What matters is you're safe, and you'll stay that way now that you're home."

His dismissal ignited a fire in me. I shoved Antonio away, anger propelling me off the bed. "You don't get to fucking say what's important!" I shoved past Massimo, my shoulder slamming into his as I stormed toward the bathroom, the fury consuming me.

I wasn't surprised to find Carmela there, the door clicking shut behind her as she leaned against it, her eyes swimming with sympathy and concern. My twin. The other half of my soul. But right now, her pity felt like poison.

"Are you just going to stand there and fucking stare at me, or do you have something to say?" I spat, my temper flaring uncontrollably. I didn't want her kindness; I wanted the pain to stop.

She crossed the small space between us and wrapped her arms around me, pulling me into her warmth. It was all I needed. The dam inside me broke, and I crumpled, my sobs echoing off the tiled walls as I buried my face in her shoulder.

"I thought I lost you, Cee." Her voice was thick with tears, and the use of my nickname only made the flood worse. "What happened? One minute you were at the bar... the next..." She drew a shaky breath, her hold on me tightening as if afraid I might disappear again.

"I just wanted to feel in control for once," I whispered, my voice breaking with the weight of everything I'd kept bottled up. "Massimo is always running people off, and Beckett... he wasn't intimidated by who we are. It was thrilling... I didn't realize it was all a game at first." I pulled back, swiping angrily at the tears on my cheeks. "But then something changed. I fell in love with him, Carmela."

"Seriously, Cee?" She stepped back, disbelief etched on her face. "Do you hear yourself? I'm pretty sure what you think is love is just Stockholm syndrome. That man is a monster, not a hero. A few days away from him, and you'll see that."

Her words hit like a slap, igniting a rage so intense it burned through the numbness. I jabbed my finger into her chest, my voice trembling with fury. "You don't know how I feel. Beckett risked everything to save me. And you're right, he isn't the hero I wanted… but he was the monster I needed. Now, my heart—what's left of it—beats unevenly because of him."

Carmela's face softened, her hand hovering over the door-knob as if she wanted to reach out but didn't know how. "Just tell me how I can help you, Celestina. I don't know what to do."

The desperation in her eyes, the helplessness in her voice, twisted the knife deeper. I scoffed, bitter laughter spilling out as I turned away. "There is nothing you can do to fix this. Nothing anyone can do." My hands moved to the hem of Beckett's shirt, the last piece of him I had. I pulled it over my head, the fabric falling to the floor like a discarded memory. I turned on the shower, the icy spray hitting my skin, sharp and punishing.

"There is absolutely nothing you can do to rid me of the pain I feel… there is no gluing my soul or taping my carnage heart together ever again."

The water beat down on me, mingling with my tears, and I stood there, letting the cold needle into my bones, wishing it could numb the agony tearing me apart from the inside.

My thoughts strayed to Beckett. Somewhere along the way, I'd fallen for my captor—and he'd fallen for me. At least, I was pretty sure he had, even *if* he hadn't said so. I squeezed my eyes closed, and like a demon, I conjured him up.

We had slipped into a dangerous rhythm. He was the hunter, and I was his prey. Before I knew it, he was in front of me, his hand wrapping around my throat, pinning me to the wall. His grip wasn't gentle—it never was. My breath came in short gasps as I struggled to take in enough air.

"Come to watch me, sugar?" His voice was low and gravelly, sending shivers down my spine.

His pet name for me washed over my skin, eliciting goose-flesh to erupt.

My skin prickled under the weight of his pet name, goose-bumps rising despite the heat between us. "Maybe I came to kill you," I rasped out, my words choked as I fought for breath.

Beckett pressed his knee between my legs and leaned against me.

His knee pushed between my legs, his body pressing harder against mine. "Unless strangling my cock with that pretty little pussy of yours is your plan to kill me, I think I'm safe."

I wanted to hate him. I did hate him. But my body betrayed me every single time. His hand slipped under the cotton shirt I was wearing—his shirt, because he'd kidnapped me with nothing but a skimpy dress and heels. And like always, he ripped it right off me, the sound of fabric tearing filling the small space. Beckett has destroyed more shirts than I could count.

"You're going to run out of shirts if you keep doing that."

The sound of Carmela knocking on the door stirred me from the nightmare of my shattered heart and I turned off the water. "What?"

"You okay?"

I swallowed hard, wiping my face even though it was impossible to tell if the wetness was from the shower or my own tears. "Yeah," I croaked, though the lie felt heavier on my tongue than the silence that followed. I stared at my discarded shirt on the floor, a ghost of him clinging to the fabric. It wasn't just the shirt he had torn apart, it was me. And no matter how many times I tried to shake him off, he was always there, lurking in the corners of my mind, filling the cracks I couldn't hide.

"Yeah," I repeated, my voice hollow as I pulled the towel around my shaking body. But the truth hung in the air, as thick and suffocating as the steam in the room—I was not okay. I wasn't sure I ever would be again.

one

CELESTINA

NINETY-ONE DAYS, three hours, twenty-seven minutes, and thirty-eight seconds.

It seemed like a blink of an eye, but the mark left was indelible. My eyes locked onto the tiny stick in my trembling hand, a stark symbol of how my world had unraveled. My fingers went numb as I tossed it into the trash. It clattered against the metal. The sound was eerily final. I turned on the faucet and shoved my hands under the scalding water, desperate to feel something other than this hollow ache. The heat seared my skin, but the pain did nothing to cleanse the turmoil that had taken root inside me.

Three months. Three months since I had given my heart to a monster, and he had vanished from my life as if I'd been nothing to him. After days of relentless pleading and anger, Massimo finally broke down and told me what happened that day. Tito found me at Beckett's house, barely conscious and covered in blood. Manuel Costa had sent his men to kill us both. Beckett's defiance had nearly cost him his life. And for weeks, I believed it had.

I clung to that grief, let it wrap around me like armor. Because believing he was dead was easier than accepting the truth: he was alive, and he hadn't come for me.

My hands gripped the edge of the sink, the tears falling hot and fast. I'd let myself fall for him, believing he saw something more in me than just a pawn in this twisted game. And now, I was left with a constant, unrelenting reminder of what we'd been and what I'd lost.

"Cee, you in there?" Carmela's voice cut through my thoughts, soft and cautious. I didn't respond. The door creaked open, and I winced as she stepped inside, her presence filling the small space. Her gaze swept over the bathroom, and her eyes widened when they landed on the discarded pregnancy test box on the counter.

"Shit," she whispered, her voice filled with shock.

"Yeah. Shit." I turned away, wiping the tears from my cheeks, trying to pull myself together as she moved closer.

She slid her arms around me, resting her head on my shoulder, our reflections merging in the mirror. Two faces, identical yet so different. Hers filled with concern, mine a mask of pain and confusion.

"Well? What's the result?"

"Positive," I breathed, the word heavy with all the fear and uncertainty swirling inside me.

She let out a long, shaky breath. "Maybe this is a good thing."

"A good thing?" I laughed, a bitter sound that echoed off the tiled walls. "How is being a single mother at twenty-three a good thing, Carmela? God, why does everyone in this family end up with babies out of wedlock? It's like a curse or something."

"Stop that," she said firmly. "You know damn well you won't be alone in this. And there's no curse. I'm not pregnant, and neither is Madison."

"Ugh… you know what I mean." I waved a hand, dismissing her logic. "What am I supposed to tell this baby? 'Hey, your daddy kidnapped me, but we fell in love, and then he disappeared after nearly dying for me.' That's not exactly going to win me mother of the year."

"We don't seem to have the best of luck picking men, do we?" Carmela squeezed me gently, and I thought back to the painful confession she'd made shortly after I came home. Carlisle's idiocy when it came to my sister was almost laughable. Almost. He kept pushing her away yet terrified every guy who dared to show interest in her. It was like watching someone try to hold onto water—it slipped through his fingers, and he didn't even realize what he was losing.

"I guess not." I pulled away, the fatigue settling over me like a heavy blanket. "Can you keep this little predicament between us? I'm not ready to deal with our brothers. Massimo is going to lose his shit."

"I think you're wrong," Carmela said, shrugging, "but I won't tell them. You need a plan, though. You won't be able to hide it for long."

She was right, of course. My clothes were already starting to feel tight. Every morning, I'd stare at my reflection, tracing the barely noticeable curve, wondering how much longer I could pretend everything was normal.

"I'll tell them after I see a doctor," I said, the words tasting bitter on my tongue. I followed Carmela out of the bathroom and down the stairs. The house was quiet, too quiet, and my heart thudded painfully in my chest as we stepped into the living room.

Antonio was sitting on the couch, his gaze lifting as we entered. He looked so at ease, his smile warm as he stood and crossed the room to envelop me in a hug.

"Are you feeling better?" he asked, his voice laced with genuine concern. I knew he was referring to the episode at dinner last night. The nausea that had gripped me, the way I'd barely made it to the bathroom before vomiting. It was the moment I could no longer deny what was happening to me.

"I'm fine," I lied, forcing a smile. "It must have been something I ate."

"Where's Rachel and the baby?" I asked, eager to shift the focus away from me.

"With Madison." His smile widened, lighting up his face. "She needed help picking out a dress, apparently. I offered to keep him, but Rachel said I earned a guy's day, whatever that means."

Seeing him like this, so happy and content, softened something in me. Antonio had been through hell, and yet here he was, thriving. Being a dad suited him, and every time he talked about his family, he seemed to glow from the inside out.

"Well, then, why are you here?" I teased gently. "Call Massimo and the others. I'm sure they'd be happy to join you."

Antonio laughed, a deep, rich sound that wrapped around me like a hug. But I could still see the worry in his eyes, the way he studied me like he was trying to piece together a puzzle.

I wasn't ready to tell him yet, to shatter the fragile peace we'd managed to build since I came back. For now, I'd keep this secret to myself, even as it grew harder to hide with every passing day.

He cocked an eyebrow at me, his voice low and serious. "I didn't want to leave."

The unspoken words weighed heavily, twisting something deep inside me. He didn't want to leave *me*. My chest tightened with frustration. Every day felt like I was living the same damn nightmare on repeat. Everyone tiptoed around me like I was made of glass, like I might shatter at the slightest touch.

"What you mean is you didn't want to leave *me*," I snapped, the bitterness thick in my throat. "I don't need a babysitter, Antonio. It's been three months. I think I'm safe now."

"You won't be safe until that motherfucker is taken down," he said, his tone steely. His protective nature, usually a comfort, now felt like a noose tightening around my neck.

"Have you found him?" I shrugged, trying to seem indifferent. "Last I heard, he was a ghost."

"Tito assures us he's looking, as are we. It's only a matter of time before that cockroach crawls out from under his rock."

"Yeah, well, I'm not going to stay hidden until then." I grabbed my bag from the table, my fingers trembling with pent-up frustration. "In fact, we're going out. Come on, Carmela."

My sister's eyes widened, darting between Antonio and me, uncertainty written all over her face. "Um…sure."

"Where are you going?" Antonio's voice was tight with anxiety. "You need a guard with you, Cee. Please don't fight me on that."

"Fine," I relented with a sigh. "We're only going to the casino. I need a drink."

I wasn't going to be drinking anything other than soda water, but he didn't need to know that. Antonio followed us to the door, stopping just short of stepping outside.

"You call me if you have any issues. I'll let Alex know you're on your way. Please, go straight there and come straight back. I couldn't handle it if something happened to you or Carmela."

His voice cracked, and the worry in his eyes broke through my anger, softening it. I sighed, the fight draining out of me. "You're right. I'm sorry, Antonio. I know I wasn't the only one who suffered when I was taken. Straight there and back, I promise."

"I love you, Cee." He pulled me into a tight hug, his warmth seeping into my skin, grounding me. "I hate that you're still hurting."

I looked up at him, sensing the ache in my chest deepen. "Then put me out of my misery and tell me where he is."

"You know I can't." Antonio stepped back, his jaw tight with frustration. "You need to forget about Beckett Heart."

A bitter laugh escaped me. "That's easier said than done."

I brushed past him, Carmela trailing behind me, and headed down the stairs to one of the many SUVs parked outside. The moment I positioned myself in the driver's seat, I allowed my head to droop against the steering wheel, the pressure of everything pressing on me like a suffocating blanket.

"You okay?" Carmela's voice was gentle, her hand resting lightly on my arm.

I lifted my head, meeting her worried gaze. "No, but I'll figure it out at some point." I started the engine, the car's low rumble filling the silence as I navigated the drive. My mind drifted, unbidden, to the last time I'd seen Beckett.

"I'm sorry I can't be the man for you." His voice had been so soft, filled with a sorrow I didn't understand. He'd brushed a loose strand of hair from my cheek, his thumb lingering on my lips as if trying to memorize the feel of them.

"You could be," I'd whispered, stepping closer, my heart aching as tears threatened to spill.

"No, Celestina. I..." He'd closed his eyes, shaking his head. "Please, just stay here. Don't open the door or turn on the lights. Only I know the code to the door. I'll come for you when it's safe."

But he hadn't. And I was still waiting.

"Hey." Carmela's hand brushed against my arm, pulling me back to the present. "You sure you want to go out?"

I glanced out the windshield, seeing Antonio watching us from the front steps, his expression torn between worry and resignation. "Yeah. I need to move on, and staying hidden isn't doing me or anyone else any good."

"Let's go to Velvet, then maybe do some shopping," Carmela suggested, her voice deliberately light.

We rode in silence, the unspoken weight of everything hanging between us. As we pulled into the parking lot, I turned to her, needing to distract myself from the whirlpool of emotions threatening to pull me under. "How about you? Are you okay being around Carlisle?"

Her face flushed, and she looked away, pretending to rummage through her bag. "Um… yeah. Actually…" She bit her lip, her cheeks turning pink. "I've kind of been seeing someone else, but it's new and neither of us wants the headache of the family getting involved. You know how the boys can be."

"Yeah, I sure do." I sighed, shaking my head. "They scare off everyone who comes within a two-foot radius of us, which is why I left with Beckett that night. Look where that got me."

"I wish they'd just tell you where he is. I don't get all the secrecy."

I shrugged, staring at the dashboard. I suspected it had something to do with their efforts to bring down Manuel Costa, but I couldn't be sure. "Let's forget about that for now. Tell me about your mystery man. Someone I know?" I raised an eyebrow, trying to lighten the mood.

"Ah… maybe." Carmela's eyes darted around the parking lot, her nervousness making my own anxiety spike.

A realization hit me like a bolt of lightning, and I turned to her, my mouth dropping open. "Holy shit. Massimo is going to kill you."

"Shit." Her eyes widened. "How'd you figure it out?"

"You two argue all the time. I swear you're either going to kill each other or fuck each other's brains out."

"Well…" She giggled, her cheeks brightening. "Definitely not killing each other."

"Oh my God, you slut." I laughed, the sound bubbling up unexpectedly. "Does he treat you well?"

"Yes… but he's worried about how Massimo will react."

"Understandable. Our brothers can be hotheads. Even if he helped save Catarina, he's still kind of an outsider."

Carmela shrugged as she pulled open the door, and my heart skipped a beat when I saw who was waiting. The man we'd been talking about appeared around the corner, his eyes lighting up when he saw her. He smiled politely at me, but it was clear his focus was entirely on Carmela.

"She's here. Yep… I'll let you know." He pocketed his phone, his grin widening. "Ladies. That was your keeper ensuring you made it. Carmela, can I speak with you privately for a moment?"

The blush on her cheeks told me everything I needed to know. "Seriously, you two… you need to come clean so you can be public. Secrecy shit sucks."

"She figured it out." Carmela shrugged, giving Alex a playful smile despite the tension. "Come here and give me a kiss. Maybe she's right. We should just tell Massimo."

"Tell Massimo what?"

Carmela froze, her expression morphing from playful to panic in an instant. I pressed a hand over my mouth, desperately trying to smother my laughter. She looked like a deer caught in headlights, and I couldn't help but find the situation almost comical despite the impending explosion.

"Oh, for fuck's sake," I blurted out, unable to hold it back any longer. "She and Alex are dating."

"Excuse me?" Massimo's voice was a low, dangerous growl as he turned his steely glare toward Carmela. "Is that right?"

"Yes, it is… but at least I'm not pregnant." Her voice cracked as she shot me a look filled with hurt and betrayal before storming off, tears spilling down her cheeks.

My heart sank, and I pinched the bridge of my nose, feeling the regret settle like a stone in my stomach. "Fuck."

"Fuck is right," Massimo muttered, his voice tight with barely contained fury. "My wife is keeping secrets from me, my sister is sleeping with my head of security, and you're pregnant with a monster's baby."

"We'll get back to the 'secrets' thing," I shot back, my voice rising with a fresh surge of anger. "But don't you dare call him a monster. If it wasn't for him, I'd be dead." I turned to Alex, feeling my protective instincts flare. "And grow a pair. Don't be like that dick behind the bar. If you like my sister, treat her with some fucking respect."

I didn't wait for a response, spinning on my heel and heading after Carmela. She'd locked herself in Massimo's office, and I could hear her muffled sobs through the heavy door. I hesitated for a moment before pushing it open and stepping inside.

She was sitting on the couch, her head buried in her hands, her shoulders shaking. Guilt twisted in my gut as I crossed the room and knelt beside her.

"I'm sorry, Carm." My voice was thick with remorse. "I lost my temper and snapped. It wasn't right, and I can't take it back, but I didn't do it to hurt you."

Carmela lifted her head, her eyes red and puffy. "I'm sorry too," she whispered, her voice quivering. "We have to stop lying to the people we love. I should have told Massimo weeks ago that Alex and I were dating."

"When did it start?"

"About a week after you came home." She wiped at her cheeks, taking a shaky breath. "He saw me arguing with Carlisle. It was bad, and Alex thought Carlisle had hurt me. He had, but not in the way Alex was thinking. Afterward, Alex told me he was attracted to me but was worried about the age difference and Massimo's reaction. I was still hurting, but he made me see I deserved more."

"You want to tell me who treated you like trash?" Massimo's voice boomed from the doorway, making us both jump. He stepped inside, his eyes blazing with protective rage, Alex trailing behind him looking tense and uneasy.

"No, I don't." Carmela's voice was firm as she stood, squaring her shoulders. "There's no point in dragging up old shit. Let's just let it go, and I'll chalk it up to being young and desperate. But Massimo, I like Alex." Her eyes softened as she looked at the man in question, a small, genuine smile curving her lips.

Massimo's jaw clenched as Alex moved to stand beside her, wrapping an arm around her waist and pulling her close. "Seriously? You're acting like your friend isn't good enough for me."

"No one is." Massimo's eyes narrowed, his gaze zeroing in on Alex's hand on Carmela's waist. "But if I had to pick someone, it'd be him. Still, I don't want to see or hear about it. I'm hanging on by a thread, wishing I could snap his neck because I can't look at him without thinking about him defiling you."

"Great. No discussion about our active sex life," Carmela deadpanned.

"Carm, please," Alex groaned, his face turning crimson. "I'd like to wake up tomorrow."

"God, the visual that just popped into my head." Massimo shuddered, shaking his head. "I think I need to bleach my brain." He turned to me, his expression shifting from disgusted to concerned in an instant. "Now, you. Let's talk about this other bomb I just got hit with. You're pregnant."

I swallowed hard, biting my lip as I nodded. "Yeah."

"Beckett's?" Massimo took two steps forward and pulled me into his arms, holding me tight.

I jerked away, my voice sharp with hurt and frustration. "Of course, it's his. Who the hell else would it be?"

"I'm sorry." He ran a hand through his hair, looking at me with a mixture of sorrow and frustration. "I just needed to be sure. Well, this changes things. We need to have a family meeting, Celestina. I think it's time you understood why we've kept things from you."

My heart pounded against my ribs, a tiny tendril of hope threading through the dark uncertainty that had settled within me for months. I looked up at him, my voice trembling. "You know where he is." It wasn't a question—I'd suspected for a long time that my brother held the key to finding Beckett, but for reasons I couldn't understand, he kept that information from me.

Massimo nodded, his grip on my arms tightening. "I do. But the reason I haven't told you isn't because I wanted to hurt you, Cee. It's because he asked me not to."

I was momentarily speechless, and I stared at him, my mind racing. "He asked you not to tell me?" My voice was a whisper, disbelief and confusion swirling inside me.

CELESTINA

MY HEART TWISTED PAINFULLY at Massimo's confession. Beckett had asked him not to tell me where he was—just another confirmation that what we'd had was all in my head. The weight of it all bore down on me, crushing whatever hope I'd been clinging to. I wiped away a stray tear and pushed my shoulders back, forcing strength into my posture even as my insides crumbled.

"I see," I murmured, my voice flat, devoid of emotion.

"Hey." Massimo pulled me against his chest, his embrace strong and reassuring, but I barely felt it. "It's not like that. Beckett knows Manuel is looking for him. He doesn't want to risk your safety any more than it already is."

"And by staying away, he's accomplishing what, exactly?" I scoffed, the bitterness clawing its way up my throat. "The only thing I see is that he's breaking my heart, Massimo. I'm pregnant by a man who doesn't want me. I'm twenty-three years old, with no job, and about to be a single mom. No, staying away to protect me is worse than risking my life to prove what we had was real, but it doesn't matter. Nothing but this baby does." I pressed my hand against my flat stomach and took a deep, shaky breath. "Excuse me, I need to use the restroom."

I slipped out from under his arm and hurried to the bathroom, barely making it inside before the tears I'd been holding back burst free. Locking myself inside the stall, I crumbled, my body shaking with the force of my sobs. Every emotion I'd bottled up—fear, anger, heartbreak—poured out, leaving me feeling hollow and exhausted.

"Celestina?" Catarina's voice echoed softly through the empty restroom. "Come out, baby sis. I need to see you're all right with my own eyes."

I wiped my face with a piece of toilet paper and unlocked the stall door. Catarina stood by the sink, her arms folded protectively over her swollen belly, her expression a mix of concern and love. She opened her arms to me, and I didn't hesitate. I fell into her embrace, burying my face in her shoulder, my tears soaking her shirt

"It's going to be okay, sweet girl." She stroked my hair, her voice gentle and soothing. I leaned against her belly, feeling the faint movements of her baby, a reminder of the life growing inside me too. "I know what you're feeling right now, and I know deep down, things will work out as they're supposed to."

"How do you know, Cat?" I whispered, my voice breaking. "Your man came after you…mine ran." I pulled back slightly, placing my hand on her baby bump. "You got your happily ever after."

"Sure, but at what cost?" She sighed, guilt flashing in her eyes. "It's my fault you were taken. If I hadn't run off like a spoiled brat, Manuel Costa's brother wouldn't be dead, and you wouldn't have been taken. The blame lies solely on me, and for that, I'm so sorry."

"It isn't your fault." I shook my head, taking a step back. "It's that bastard and his brother's fault. Donny did the world a favor when he ended that fucker's life."

"Yeah…" Catarina sighed heavily. "But in doing so, he started a war. One I fueled with my own fears. If I had just faced my feelings a long time ago, maybe you wouldn't be in the women's room crying because your heart is breaking."

"Let's agree to disagree, okay? Throwing blame around won't change the past." I forced a weak smile, hoping to ease some of the guilt weighing on her.

"All right." Catarina tilted her head, studying me closely. "But I need you to promise me something." She placed her hand protectively over her belly. "Don't let the sadness pull you under. You're pregnant, which means you have to take care of yourself, for your baby's sake."

The door swung open, and Carmela stepped inside, her gaze immediately locking onto mine.

"You good, Cee? Donny and Massimo are out there, ready to tear down this door. I know you're hurt and scared, but you have us… your family. You won't be alone, and I promise this baby is going to be loved, no matter what."

"You're right." I nodded, taking a deep breath and straightening my shoulders. "Wallowing in heartbreak isn't going to change a damn thing. Okay. Let's get out of here. I love you two."

Catarina and Carmela wrapped me in a group hug. "We love you too, Cee."

By the time we stepped out of the bathroom, it seemed like the entire family had gathered. Everyone but Michael and Rachel was there. Madison rushed over, pulling me into a tight embrace.

"Congratulations, Celestina. This family is growing like wildfire."

I felt a pang of guilt, knowing how much Madison and Massimo wanted to get married and have a family of their own. They had been together the longest but hadn't managed to tie the knot yet. Madison had promised *Nonna* they'd get married in Sicily, but with all the chaos, it hadn't been possible.

"I feel bad. Every time things calm down, one of us is stealing your chance to have your moment. Perhaps it's time we directed our attention toward your union with Massimo. *Nonna* would understand if you got married here."

Madison's eyes clouded briefly, a shadow passing over her face, but she quickly smiled, shaking her head. "Nope. I made a promise to her, and I intend to keep it. Besides, I don't need a wedding band to know Massimo is mine. That's just a formality. When the time is right, it'll happen."

"All right, but just so you know, I was hoping to use you to keep my mind off things. Planning a wedding would be a great way to do that."

"Well, why didn't you say so? We can totally set a tentative date and plan it. Would you like to do that for me, Celestina? Would you be my wedding planner?"

Closing my eyes, I blew out a breath. Madison was doing what she always did—finding a way to help. That's who she was, the most selfless person I knew. She was the perfect match for my brooding brother.

"Yes. I would love that."

"Love what?" Massimo's deep voice interrupted, and I looked up to see him wrapping his arms around Madison's waist, pressing a kiss to her head.

"I'm going to plan your wedding."

Massimo shot Madison a look, his brow furrowing briefly before his expression softened into a smile. "Excellent. We'll come to Antonio's for dinner and discuss things tonight."

"Hey, now…not without me." Antonio draped his arm over my shoulder. "Madison is my best friend, and I am most definitely going to help."

"Actually…" Madison grinned. "I was hoping you'd be my man of honor."

My breath hitched as I watched Antonio's eyes fill with tears. He blinked rapidly, trying to hold them back.

"Are you serious?"

"Of course, silly." Madison's grin widened. "You're not just my brother-to-be, you're my best friend."

Antonio moved away from me and pulled her into his arms. I

couldn't contain my laugh when Massimo growled beside them.

"Oh, stop it, you big jerk," I teased. "That's your brother, and Madison is completely in love with you. She'd have to be to put up with you and the family drama for so long."

"Mine." Massimo pulled Madison away from Antonio and into his arms, possessiveness radiating from every inch of him. "You've got your own woman… and man at home. Go rub on them and stop touching mine."

"You ass," Madison muttered, smacking his chest.

He caught her hand and pressed his lips to hers, and we all groaned.

"Jesus… Can you two save that for when we aren't all standing here watching?" Carmela made a gagging noise, and I burst out laughing.

Massimo broke the kiss, arching a brow. "Oh…so you expect me to watch Alex maul you, but I can't do that with my woman?"

"Wait." Vincenzo's eyes narrowed as he turned to Carmela, his expression darkening. "You and Alex?" His gaze swept the room, landing on Alex standing by the entrance. "I'm going to kill him."

"Whoa there, psycho." Massimo grabbed his jacket, holding him in place. "Alex is a good man. This isn't a bad thing, Vin. He'll keep Carmela out of trouble."

Vincenzo paused, his body sagging as he exhaled. "You're okay with it?"

"Yeah. Of course, if he hurts her, you have my permission to show him how well you handle a knife."

"What?" Carmela's eyes widened. "No, you can't do that. Jesus Christ, what's wrong with this family?"

I couldn't stop laughing. My family was the textbook definition of dysfunctional. We never did things the normal way—ever. I placed my hand over my belly, a sense of calm washing over me. Being pregnant wasn't ideal, but looking at the people around me, I knew I would be okay.

"Massimo, I need a favor." My brother turned to look at me, concern in his eyes. "If you hear from Beckett, I don't want him to know."

"You don't want him to know he's going to be a father?"

"I don't want him to come back because I'm having his baby. I'd always question if he was here because he actually loves me or if it was out of a sense of duty. Despite what you think you know about him, Beckett Heart prides himself on his sense of duty. It's partly why he's not here, right? Because he thinks he's keeping me safe? Imagine what he'll do if he learns I'm carrying his baby."

"He'll come back because he thinks he has to." Madison spoke the words I knew were true in my heart.

"Ding, ding, ding." I pressed my lips together. "And I don't want that. So, promise me, Massimo. I'm your sister, so your loyalty is to me…not him."

Massimo's gaze held mine for a beat before he nodded. "Fine, but eventually, you need to let him know, Celestina. A man deserves to know he has an heir, and he owes you—whether you want to believe that or not."

"Fine… I'll cross that bridge if I ever face him again, but for now, I don't want him alerted."

"All right, enough doom and gloom." I clapped my hands. "I'm hungry. Who wants to take me to lunch?"

"I'll take her, then bring her home," Antonio volunteered. "Maybe we can go shopping after I get you fed."

"All right, keep her safe, brother." Massimo patted him on the back. *"Fino a stasera."*

"Fino a stasera. Come on, mama, let's go get you some grub."

I hugged everyone goodbye and followed Antonio toward the exit. As we passed Alex, he smiled.

"Congratulations, Celestina."

I leaned close, lowering my voice as I grabbed a handful of his balls. "If you hurt my sister, I'll strip your balls off your body and feed them to you."

Alex's eyes widened, and he swallowed hard. "Um, you think you could let go of my nuts, Celestina?"

Releasing him, I took a step back, my eyes narrowed. "Just don't hurt her."

"Don't plan on it. I'm falling for her. It's me who's in danger of getting hurt. She's like the sun. She's the light in the darkness, but if you get too close, you risk getting burned."

I blinked at his accurate assessment of my twin. She was like the sun, but he was wrong. She wouldn't burn him. She'd warm his soul for all eternity if he loved her right. Something I would never have.

"Damn, Cee." Antonio chuckled as we climbed into his SUV. "I didn't know you had a violent side. Guess you're more like Vin than I realized. I think Alex's balls shrunk a little. I'm pretty sure he nearly pissed himself."

"Carmela has been hurt before. I don't want to see it happen again."

Antonio's hands tightened on the steering wheel, his knuckles turning white. "Who hurt her?"

"Not my story to tell." I shook my head, a sad smile tugging at my lips. "She's put it behind her, and she's stronger because of it. Just trust that everything is okay now."

Antonio glanced at me with a fierce expression. "Was she hurt physically?"

"No, not physically. It was more her heart and pride that took the hit. But I swear, if it was something more, I'd be the first to throw the pebble in the pond."

"You're going to make a damn fine mother, Cee." He arched an eyebrow at me. "Your baby lucked out when God picked you to be his or her mother."

"I hope I can be as good a parent as you and Vin are. I see how you are with my nieces and nephews, and I want that for my baby."

"You'll have it, Cee. I'll make damn sure of it."

three

CELESTINA

ONE HUNDRED AND FIFTY-TWO DAYS, *nine hours, thirty-two minutes, and seventeen seconds.*

Time felt like an eternity since I'd held Beckett. Massimo hadn't been able to contact him, so for all anyone knew, he might've been dead. My brother swore he was searching, but I had my doubts. That thought made my stomach churn with bile. Pressing my palm against the tiny round bump, I took several deep breaths and closed my eyes.

"You about ready to go?" Michael stood in the doorway of my bedroom, smiling.

I forced a smile back. "As ready as I'll ever be. Any word on Manuel Costa?"

"No." Michael shook his head. "The fucker has gone to ground."

"Maybe he's finally giving up on hunting me."

Michael's face softened and his eyes became gentle. "You

know men like him don't give up, Celestina. He'll lie low and then strike when he thinks we've relaxed."

I forced a laugh. "Good thing we're never relaxed. Whatever, let's go."

We headed out of his house to his SUV.

"You sure you don't want one of the girls to go with you?" he asked as we got in.

"God, no. They'll make this into a bigger deal than I need it to be."

"And you don't think I won't? I missed out on Dante's first ultrasound. This is going to be fun for me."

"Oh, lord." I rolled my eyes, but secretly, I was grateful he was here. "Maybe I should have asked Vincenzo to come."

"That psycho?" Michael laughed. "Nope. You picked right."

When we pulled into the parking lot, Michael glanced over at me. "Any thoughts about what you want?"

I shook my head, a small smile tugging at my lips. "I don't care, as long as they're healthy."

He grinned. "Good answer."

The receptionist checked us in, and soon, we were being led back to the ultrasound room. I laughed when the nurse asked if Michael was my husband.

"Um… no. This is my brother-in-law. Daddy's away right now." I patted my belly.

"Oh. Well, it's nice you have someone with you. It makes a huge difference having support." She smiled and gestured to the table. "Hop up there, and I'll let the tech know you're ready."

Michael shot me a weird look as I climbed onto the table.

"What?" I shrugged. "I don't feel like explaining I got pregnant and dumped."

He shrugged, a smile tugging at his lips. "Fair enough."

The ultrasound tech came in, his demeanor friendly and professional. "Hi, Miss Anastasi, I'm Evan, and I'll be doing your scan today." He glanced at Michael. "And you are?"

"Uncle Michael," he said, grinning. "The baby's father is out of town, so I'm here for moral support."

"Great." Evan adjusted the monitor, then raised my shirt and squirted some gel on my abdomen. "This might be a little cold."

I jumped slightly, then laughed. "Actually, it's not bad."

"Good." He smiled. "Let's see what we've got." He moved the wand across my belly, and I gasped as the screen lit up.

"That's my baby?"

"Sure is," Evan said, his voice warm. "I'm going to get some measurements, and then we'll see if we can find out if you're having a boy or girl. Do you have a preference?"

I shook my head, my eyes glued to the screen. "I just want them to be healthy."

Michael squeezed my hand as we watched. "You're going to be an amazing mom, Cee."

Evan nodded. "Your baby is developing perfectly. Everything looks great. You ready to find out the gender?"

I held my breath, nodding.

He moved the wand around, pressing down. "Come on, little one, show us your stuff."

And then there it was, clear as day. A tiny foot kicked at the screen, and Evan smiled.

"There. It's a girl."

My eyes filled with tears as I stared at the screen, my heart swelling with a love I'd never felt before.

"A girl," I whispered, tears spilling over. "I'm having a daughter."

Michael squeezed my hand, his voice choked with emotion. "Congratulations, Cee."

Evan printed out several images and handed them to me, along with a CD of the scan.

"Thank you," I said, my voice thick with gratitude.

Michael and I headed out, the pictures clutched tightly in my hand. He glanced at me as we reached the car.

"You hungry?"

My stomach growled in response, and I laughed. "Starving."

"Let's get you a burger, then."

We headed to Gino's, and I couldn't stop smiling. For the first time in a long time, I had a flicker of hope. My daughter was going to be okay. We were going to be okay.

As we drove, Michael stiffened, glancing in the rearview mirror. "You got your seatbelt on?"

I frowned, confused. "Yeah. Why?"

"We've got a tail." He pressed a button on the steering wheel, activating the Bluetooth.

"Hey, babe. How'd—"

"Antonio, we've got a problem." Michael cut off Antonio before he could finish. "We've got a tail."

"Fuck. Where are you?"

"Just left the doctor's office, heading to Gino's. They're going to make a move."

"Hang on," Antonio growled, his voice a jagged edge of urgency slicing through the chaos. I could hear muffled voices, the harsh tone of his words like the prelude to a storm. When he came back on the line, his words were clipped and tense. "Vin's got Rachel's phone. Head to The Sapphire Dagger. He's waiting for you."

"Shit," Michael muttered, his knuckles whitening as he tightened his grip on the steering wheel. He glanced in the rearview mirror, eyes narrowed on the black SUV tailing us, its headlights glaring like the eyes of a predator. "They're going to try and force us off the road. I don't think we'll make it to Vin."

The SUV behind us lunged forward, slamming into our bumper with a sickening crunch. My body jerked forward, hands flying to the dashboard as a scream ripped from my throat, raw and terrified. The car fishtailed, tires screeching in protest as Michael fought for control, his muscles straining, the veins in his neck standing out like cords.

"You hear that, Vin?" Antonio's voice was a panicked blur on the other end of the line. "Michael, keep them off your ass. Vin is coming in hot on his bike."

The words barely registered. "Oh my God!" I cried out, bracing myself against the dashboard, my heart pounding so hard it felt like it might burst. "Antonio…" My voice was a broken whisper, trembling with fear as I clung to anything solid, anything that could keep me grounded in this nightmare.

"It's going to be okay, Cee." Michael's voice was tight, focused, but there was a tremor in it, a crack that spoke of fear he couldn't quite hide. "Vin will be here. Just hang on."

"Cee," he said, tapping my leg with one hand while his other struggled to keep the car on the road. "Open the glove box, sweetheart, and grab my gun."

"What?" My hands fumbled for the latch, fingers trembling as I pulled the compartment open. My heart stuttered when I saw the sleek, cold metal of the Glock lying there like a deadly promise.

"When did you start carrying a gun?" My voice was high-pitched, laced with panic as I picked it up, the weight of it foreign and frightening in my hand.

"After getting kidnapped and almost dying. It's one of many things I've learned to handle. Hand it to me." His words were calm, matter-of-fact, but I could see the way his jaw clenched, the way his eyes darted between the road and the rearview mirror. He was scared too, and that terrified me even more.

"I'm scared." I handed him the gun, my fingers brushing against his, cold and clammy. I glanced over my shoulder, the SUV looming behind us like a black shadow, relentless and unforgiving. "Who are they?"

Michael shot me a look, his eyes dark with a fury that made me shiver. "You know who it is, Cee. Costa isn't going to stop until he gets his revenge. We killed his brother. We ruined his plans. Now he's out for blood."

"This is insane." My voice broke, the words strangled by the lump of fear in my throat. "Oh!" I screamed as the SUV rammed into us again, the impact jarring, violent. The seatbelt bit into my shoulder, my body slamming against the side of the door. "It's broad daylight! Where the hell are the cops?"

Michael's mouth twisted into a grim smile. "We don't need them. Vin's here."

And then, like a guardian angel riding out of the abyss, Vin's black Ducati roared past my window, sleek and powerful, the rumble of its engine a battle cry in the quiet chaos of our terror. The SUV behind us clipped our bumper again, sending the car into a wild spin.

"Hold on!" Michael shouted, yanking the wheel, his body taut with the effort. The car swerved, the SUV crashing into us again, pushing us sideways. Metal screamed as the vehicles locked, and then we were spinning, spinning, until my world was a blur of colors and sound.

Time slowed to a crawl. I saw Michael's face, his jaw set, eyes blazing with defiance as he fought the wheel. I felt the car lurch, heard the shatter of glass, the roar of an engine too close, and then the gut-wrenching impact as we crashed into something solid.

Agonizing pain burst inside my chest, sharp and all-consuming. My arms wrapped instinctively around my stomach, a desperate attempt to shield my unborn daughter from the chaos around us. My screams filled the car, mingling with the terrible sound of metal crumpling, of tires screeching, of the world collapsing in on itself.

"Cee… Michael!" Antonio's voice was a lifeline, cutting through the ringing in my ears. I forced my eyes open, vision blurring as I turned to look at Michael. He was slumped over the steering wheel, blood trickling from a cut on his forehead, his chest barely moving.

"Michael!" I gasped, unbuckling my seatbelt with shaking hands. The ache in my chest was a dull throb, every breath like fire. I reached out, my hand trembling as I pressed my fingers to his throat. A sob tore through me when I felt the faint but steady beat of his pulse. "Antonio, he's unconscious. Michael…please wake up."

Panic clawed at me as I looked around, my vision swimming. The world outside the car was a twisted mess of metal and shattered glass. I couldn't see Vin; I couldn't see anyone. "Oh my God. Antonio, where's Vin? I don't see him. Please…" My voice broke, tears streaming down my face as I struggled to stay calm, to hold on to some semblance of control, but it was slipping, slipping, and I was drowning in fear.

My door was wrenched open, and I screamed, lashing out blindly, my fists connecting with something solid. A grunt of pain, a familiar curse.

"Cee… It's me. Fuck." Massimo's voice, rough and urgent, pulled me back from the edge. I sagged against him, the adrenaline draining out of me, leaving me weak and trembling.

"Massimo…Vin…I can't see him. Please…Michael needs you." The words tumbled out, desperate and pleading.

"Vin's okay, baby girl," he murmured, his arms strong and steady around me. "He and Drew took care of the two in the SUV that hit you. Come on. I need to get you in my car, so I can grab Michael."

He lifted me as if I weighed nothing, cradling me against his chest as he carried me to his SUV. I clung to him, my face buried in his shoulder, the sobs coming hard and fast, my entire body shaking with the force of them. I didn't even realize Alex was there until he was pulling me into the back seat, his arms wrapping around me, his voice a soothing murmur in my ear.

"Are you hurt?" His hands moved over me, checking for injuries, his touch gentle but firm. "Celestina, do you need a doctor?"

"I don't think so." The words were a sob, broken and raw. "Why is this happening?"

Massimo was back, helping Michael into the front seat, his movements careful but efficient. Michael's face was pale, pain etched into every line, but he was awake, his eyes finding mine in the mirror.

"You good, Cee?" His voice was a whisper, strained.

"You could have died." The thought was unbearable, the fear of losing him, of losing anyone else, too much. I hiccupped, the sobs tearing through me. "I just want this to stop."

Massimo climbed into the driver's seat, his face a mask of rage and resolve. "Drew and Vin are going to deal with the cops," he said, his words tight, controlled. He glanced back at me, his gaze softening. "You will be checked out… Michael, too. Don't fucking argue with me, Cee. That motherfucker tried to get you again. I'm done fucking around with Costa. He wants a war… Well, he just got one."

His words lingered ominously, a promise of retribution, of violence, of an end to this relentless cycle of fear. I stared at him, my heart aching, the tears still falling as I held on to Alex, held on to the only thing keeping me from completely breaking apart.

Massimo was right. This had to end. But I was so damn scared of what that ending would look like.

# four

ANTONIO WAS WAITING for us when we pulled up to his house, his jaw set in a grim line, eyes scanning the surroundings like a sentry on high alert. Michael had insisted we come here instead of the hospital, citing the added security and isolation that made it nearly impenetrable. Fort Knox had nothing on Antonio's place. It was a sanctuary, but today it felt more like a fortress holding back the chaos.

Kevin Luchasi, the family's private physician, had agreed to meet us there. He'd become a part of our tangled web after Massimo helped him with some life-altering issue shortly after we found Michael. Whatever it was, it had been serious enough for Kevin to swear his loyalty, binding himself to the family in a way few would dare. He often said my brother saved his life and that he would be in our debt until his last breath. Massimo had taken it in stride, simply saying we needed someone like Kevin, someone who could come when we called, no questions asked.

The moment we came to a stop, Antonio yanked open the

passenger door, and without a word, lifted Michael out, cradling him as if he were a child.

"Hey. Put me down, I can walk," Michael protested, but his voice was weak, and his face pale.

Antonio grunted, ignoring his words as he slammed the door shut with his hip. "Shut up, Michael. You know damn well you can't walk right now." His tone was firm, but there was an undercurrent of fear in it that made my heart ache.

Massimo slid out of the front seat, his movements brisk and controlled as he rounded the car and opened my door. "Don't argue, Cee," he said softly, scooping me up with surprising gentleness. "You're pregnant, and you were just in a car acci- dent. I'm not taking any chances with you or my niece or nephew."

I sighed, letting my head fall against his shoulder, the exhaus- tion and adrenaline leaving me weak and compliant. "It's a girl," I mumbled, feeling the truth of it wash over me again like a bittersweet wave. "I'm having a girl."

Massimo froze mid-step, his eyes widening as he stared down at me. "A girl?" His voice was a mix of awe and something else—something vulnerable that I hadn't heard in years.

"Yes… Fuck," I cursed under my breath as I remembered my bag, left behind in the wreckage. "I left all the images in the car. The video of the ultrasound, everything."

His eyes darkened with worry, but he managed a small smile. "I'll call Vin and tell him to grab it. Another girl," he muttered, his voice growing gentler as he resumed walking. "We're screwed. Boys, we can handle…but you women wrap us around your fingers. Two baby girls to look after." His voice hardened as he turned to Alex, who was following closely behind. "Call the guys in. We need to make a plan. Costa isn't going to touch another hair on my family's head. He wants to play with the big boys? Well, he got his wish."

Inside, the house was buzzing with an undercurrent of tension. Everyone was there—Madison, Rachel, Carmela, Catarina, Danny, and Riley—all gathered in the foyer, their faces pale and strained. The air was thick with worry, and the moment we entered, all eyes were on us.

"Oh my God, Cee!" Carmela rushed forward, her hand trembling as she reached for me, her eyes wide with fear. "Are you okay?"

"Let's get her settled, Carmela," Massimo said gently but firmly, guiding me through the crowd. "Anyone heard from Dr. Luchasi?"

"He said he'd be here in ten minutes," Danny replied. His arms were wrapped protectively around my oldest sister's shoulders. His gaze shifted to Michael, his eyes narrowing. "What the fuck happened?"

"No." I lifted a hand, my voice sharp. "Don't you dare. This is not his fault, so don't take that fucking tone with him."

Catarina closed her eyes, her face drawn and weary. "It's mine."

"Fuck that, Cat." My voice was hard, but it cracked at the edges, the fear and anger boiling over. "The only person to blame here is Manuel Costa. As soon as his brother died, he saw an opening." I looked around, a sudden panic gripping me as I realized someone was missing. "Where's Leo?"

The sound of a baby's cry echoed from the living room, and I pushed past Massimo, nearly stumbling as I rushed toward it. My heart clenched when I saw my nephew in his car seat, his tiny fists waving in the air. Everything else fell away as I unbuckled him, lifting him into my arms. His warmth, his soft coos against my chest, were like a magic potion on my shattered soul. I pressed my face against his head, inhaling the sweet, innocent scent of him. "Getting big on me, little guy?" I whispered, kissing his soft hair. "You make everything better."

"You look good with him," Danny said, his voice breaking the spell. He smiled at me, his eyes crinkling at the corners. "You and your sister make beautiful babies."

I smiled back, though it felt strained, a pale imitation of the joy I'd once known. "I hope you make more of them."

"Shh…" He glanced over at Catarina, his expression softening as he watched her. "Don't say that too loud. Cat hasn't forgiven me for putting a big baby in her yet. She'd cut off my cock if she thought I wanted another right now."

"Do you?"

"Hell yeah." His voice was quiet, but there was a fierce, tender pride in it. "I love that woman, and this is the best gift I could ever get, aside from marrying her."

I felt a pang of longing, a deep, aching sadness that settled in my chest like a stone. I looked at Leo, his tiny face peaceful against my shoulder, and then at Danny, his love for my sister so clear it was almost tangible. It was everything I wanted, everything I was terrified I'd never have.

Riley rounded the corner then, Gia in her arms. My niece wriggled, her little legs kicking, demanding to be put down. The moment Riley set her down, she toddled over to me, her tiny steps wobbly but determined. I gasped, my heart swelling with pride and shock.

"She's walking?" I breathed, my eyes wide as I watched her plop down in front of me, a beaming smile on her face.

"Trying to." Riley laughed with a voice weary but filled with love. "And it's exhausting. She's either running or sleeping, nothing in between." She sat down beside me, taking my hand in hers, her touch warm and reassuring. "How are you, really?"

I glanced around at the people I loved, the people who were all here because of me, because I'd dragged them into this nightmare. "Someone wants to kill me," I said flatly, a bitter laugh escaping my lips. "I'm an unwed mother-to-be. I'd say I'm just peachy."

Before Riley could respond, the door opened, and Dr. Kevin Luchasi strode in, his expression serious but calm. He took one look at Michael and shook his head. "You're one indestructible motherfucker. Get over here and let me check you out."

Michael muttered something incoherent, but I could see the relief in his eyes as he let Antonio help him up. Rachel hovered nearby, their baby son cradled in her arms, her face pale with worry.

Kevin turned to me, his gaze softening as he set his medical bag down. "All right, missy," he said with a gentle smile. "Let's see how you're doing. I hear you're adding a little ray of sunshine to the family."

I rolled my eyes, but I couldn't help the small smile that tugged at my lips. "Something tells me this baby will be anything but sunshine, Doc. If she's anything like my sister and me… well, the men in this family are in trouble."

He chuckled, his eyes twinkling as he pressed the stethoscope to my chest, then moved it to my belly. The room fell silent as he listened, his face thoughtful and intent. After a few minutes, he looked up, his smile reassuring.

"No pain or cramping?"

"None so far," I said, my voice steadier than I felt. "Do I need to go to the ER?" Fear spiked through me, sharp and sudden, making my voice tremble. "Is my baby okay?"

"I don't think so," he said, his tone soothing. "You may be sore, but I think you're in the clear. Just rest for a day or two, take it easy."

"She'll rest," Vincenzo's voice cut through the room like a whip. He stood in the doorway, his face a mask of barely contained fury. "She's not leaving this house until the threat is gone."

I pushed myself up, anger flaring hot and fierce. "You can't lock me up like a prisoner, Vin."

He took a step forward, his eyes blazing. "Manuel sent men to kidnap you, Cee. Do you know what they would have done to you? To your baby?"

Tears welled in my eyes, a mix of anger, fear, and guilt. "I should never have left with him," I whispered, the weight of my choices crushing me.

Before anyone could say more, I bolted, running up the stairs, needing to escape, needing space to breathe. I couldn't face their anger, their fear. I couldn't bear to see the disappointment in their eyes. I slammed the door to my room, collapsing onto the bed as sobs racked my body.

The door clicked softly, and I felt the bed dip beside me. Carmela's arms wrapped around me, her presence a temporary Band-Aid on my shattered nerves.

"You're scared, Cee, and I get it. But you're still in love with Beckett. I know you are. Our hearts latch onto who they want, and no matter how hard we try, they don't let go."

I turned to face her, tears blurring my vision. "Are you saying you're still pining after a man who didn't deserve you?"

Carmela sighed, brushing a tear from my cheek. "This isn't about me. It's about you and my niece. I know you're terrified of doing this alone, but you're not alone. Everyone downstairs would die for you."

She placed her hand gently on my belly. "And her. We already love her, Cee. So please, stay here, let us keep you safe. Antonio and Michael, they'll protect you. This place is a fortress."

I couldn't hold back the sob that tore from me. The pain and fear was crashing down like a tidal wave. Carmela held me, her touch soothing, her love wrapping around me like a cocoon. I hated this, hated the fear, the danger, but I hated more that my daughter was being born into this world, a world where shadows of death loomed over every joy, every hope.

My stomach growled, loud and demanding, breaking the tension. Carmela laughed softly, the sound a welcome relief.

"Hungry?"

"Yeah," I admitted, managing a weak smile. "We got interrupted on our way to lunch."

She kissed my forehead and stood. "I'll get someone to bring you food. You stay here and rest, okay?"

"Actually, I think I'll take a shower."

"Perfect. By the time you're done, we'll have a feast ready for you."

I watched her go, the door clicking shut behind her. For a moment, I just sat there, the silence settling around me like a heavy blanket. Then I stood, heading to the adjoining bathroom, stripping off my clothes as I went. I turned on the shower, stepping under the spray, the hot water cascading over me, washing away the grime, the fear, the tears.

I pressed my hands against the cool tiles, letting the water pound against my back, my head bowed. I wanted to disappear, to fade away into the steam and the water, to forget, just for a little while, that my life was a mess, that I was bringing a child into a world that was anything but safe.

But I couldn't. I couldn't leave my family, couldn't let them suffer the way we all had when Catarina ran away. I'd tasted love, and now all I had was the bitter aftertaste of loss. The man I loved was gone, and I was left with nothing but memories and a future filled with uncertainty.

I stood there for a long time, the water cooling as my tears finally dried. I would be strong. For my daughter, for my family, I would be strong. Even if it killed me.

five

CELESTINA

TWO HUNDRED SEVENTY-THREE DAYS, *four hours, and sixteen seconds.*

That's how long I'd been pregnant, and each second seemed to stretch into an eternity. If someone had told me being nine months pregnant would be this exhausting, I would have thought twice about ever having sex. Okay…that's a lie. But carrying a tiny human was no joke. Sleep was a distant memory, my ankles were permanently swollen, and the constant need to pee was an unending torment. Pregnancy wasn't just hard; it was brutal. And being trapped inside my brother's fortress of a house made it feel a thousand times worse.

"Please," I begged, my voice cracking with desperation as I looked between my brothers, my eyes pleading. "I need to get out of this house. Just for a few minutes, Antonio. I've followed your damn rules for the last four months. My doctor has made special trips here to check on me, and I haven't been beyond the backyard. Once this baby arrives, I won't have the freedom to do anything."

Massimo sighed, his fingers raking through his hair in frustration. The sight of him, usually so composed and in control, now looking weary and strained, tugged at my heart. But I couldn't relent. Not this time. "You know it's too dangerous, Cee. Manuel has put out a million-dollar bounty on you."

I threw my hands in the air, a frustrated groan escaping my lips. "This sucks."

"I know, and I'm sorry," he uttered, his voice softening, but the steely resolve in his eyes didn't waver. "But we can't risk your safety this close to delivery."

My frustration boiled over, tears stinging my eyes as I struggled to rein in my emotions. "What if it's just to The Sapphire Dagger? He wouldn't be stupid enough to try something there, would he?"

"Too risky. It puts you out in the open," he replied, his tone leaving no room for negotiation.

"Fine," I huffed, throwing up my hands in exasperation. "I'll just be upstairs in my room… doing nothing."

I turned and stormed up the stairs, the sound of their voices following me, but I didn't care. It felt like the walls were closing in on me, every room a prison cell. Once inside my room, I pulled out my phone and dialed Carmela, my fingers trembling.

"Hey, Cee, what's up?" Her voice, warm and familiar, was a balm to my frayed nerves.

"I need to get out of this house, Ela," I pleaded, the desperation raw in my voice. "I'm losing my mind."

She sighed heavily, and I could almost see her pinching the bridge of her nose, weighing the risks in her head. "You know it's dangerous, Cee. What if someone sees you, and you're taken?"

"Am I going to be held captive in my own house even after this baby is born? Please, Ela. I just need to get out. Take me to Vin's restaurant. We'll be safe there."

Silence stretched between us, and I held my breath, my heart pounding in my chest. I could almost hear her thoughts, the conflict tearing at her. "How am I supposed to get you out? Antonio watches you like a hawk."

"I have a plan. Just come over. He won't think anything of you spending time with me."

"I'm going to regret this…" she muttered, but I could hear the resolve in her voice. "Fine. I'll be there in twenty minutes."

I hung up, my heart racing with a mixture of excitement and anxiety. The plan was reckless, but I was suffocating in this house. I needed to breathe, even if it was just for a little while.

I made my way down to the living room and headed straight for Antonio's office. He'd moved his workspace to the house after Michael was attacked, and he'd been there almost non-stop since. I eased the door open, peering around the frame, my pulse quickening.

"Stop snooping and come in, Cee," Antonio called out, his tone gruff but not unkind.

I stepped inside, surprised to see Carlisle standing there. His presence was a reminder of past hurts, a wound that had barely scabbed over. He looked at me, his eyes lingering just a moment too long, and I felt a flare of anger rise up, bitter and sharp.

"Shouldn't you be at the bar?" I asked, my voice colder than I intended.

He shrugged, an indifferent smile playing on his lips. "Had to drop something off for your brother."

Ignoring him, I turned to Antonio, my resolve hardening. "Since I can't leave, I need you to run to the store, please."

Antonio's eyebrows shot up in surprise, his gaze narrowing. "Get one of the guards to go."

"I'm not asking them to get me ice cream," I shot back, giving him my best puppy-dog eyes.

"Ice cream?" He sounded incredulous, like I'd just asked him to fetch the moon. "Seriously, Cee? Call Michael or Rachel. They can pick it up."

"Please…" I stuck out my lip, making my voice as pitiful as possible. "Your niece wants Rocky Road."

He stared at me for a long moment, his expression torn between exasperation and amusement, then tossed his pen down in defeat. "Fine. But only because I feel bad for keeping you locked up. Carlisle, tell Massimo I'll have someone cover for me tomorrow."

"Nice seeing you again, Celestina," Carlisle said as he walked past me, his smirk infuriating. "Tell your sister hello."

"Fat chance, you piece of shit," I muttered under my breath, my eyes narrowing as he disappeared down the hall.

Antonio's eyes widened, his voice tense with concern. "Please tell me he's not the one who hurt Carmela, because I'll kill him, Massimo's friend or not."

I shook my head, a bitter smile tugging at my lips. "Let it go, Antonio. Carmela's got a good man now, one who actually loves her."

He nodded reluctantly, pulling me into a quick hug before heading out the door. "Promise me you'll behave while I'm gone."

"Of course. What kind of trouble can I get into alone?"

I watched his car disappear down the driveway, a sigh of relief escaping me. Now, I just needed Carmela to get here before Antonio realized what was happening. Five minutes later, her black SUV pulled up.

I waddled down the steps as fast as my pregnant body would allow, relief flooding through me as I climbed into the passenger seat. "Thank God."

"Where's Antonio?" Carmela asked, glancing around nervously.

"Ice cream run. Let's go before he catches my prison break."

Just as she put the car in drive, the back door flew open, and Carlisle slipped in, a grin spreading across his face.

"Where are you two off to?" he asked, leaning back and crossing his arms, the easy confidence in his voice grating on my nerves.

"Get the fuck out of my car," Carmela snapped, her eyes flashing with anger.

He shook his head, still smiling. "No can do. I saw Antonio leave and got curious. Where are you going?"

"Just drive, Carmela," I urged, feeling my pulse quicken. "He's already here. If the guards haven't called Antonio, they will soon."

Carmela hesitated, then hit the gas, the tires squealing as we sped down the drive. We barely made it through the gate before one of the guards came running down the hill, waving frantically. "Shit," Carmela muttered, nearly scraping the side of the car on the gate as it swung open.

"This is a bad idea," Carlisle said, his tone suddenly serious. "You need to go back."

"Shut up, Carlisle," I snapped, my voice shaking. "You're the one who decided to stick your nose in."

Carmela glanced at me, her face pale, eyes wide with worry. "Do you really want to do this, Cee? We can go back."

I shook my head, the tears I'd been holding back threatening to spill over. "I can't stay in that house anymore. I'm losing my mind, Ela."

She nodded, her jaw tightening, determination settling in her features. "All right, then. Let's do this."

We drove in silence, tension thick and oppressive, every bump and turn sending jolts of anxiety through me. Just as we turned off the main road, a chill ran down my spine. Something wasn't right. I scanned the street, my gut screaming at me to turn around. "Ela—" I started, but the words died in my throat as a black SUV barreled toward us, slamming into our side.

The world exploded into chaos, a deafening crash of metal against metal, glass shattering, the car lurching violently. I screamed, my hands flying to my belly as we were tossed around like rag dolls. Pain shot through me, sharp and unrelenting, and I clutched at my stomach, terror ripping through me.

"Carmela! Carlisle!" I cried, my voice hoarse and broken as the car finally came to a stop, wedged against a guardrail. Blood trickled down my face, blurring my vision as I tried to move. "Carlisle!" I turned, but he was gone, the back door hanging open, a dark smear of blood where he'd been thrown out.

"Fuck!" I gasped, every breath a struggle as I tried to unbuckle my seatbelt. My sister hung limp beside me, her head lolling at an unnatural angle. "Carm, please wake up!" I sobbed, reaching for her, my hand trembling uncontrollably.

The door was yanked open, and I was dragged out, my feet scraping against the concrete as I struggled to stand. I screamed as I was thrown to the ground, my arms wrapping protectively around my belly.

"Please," I whimpered, my voice cracking. "Don't hurt me. I'm pregnant."

The masked man ignored me, his cold eyes scanning me briefly before turning to his partner. "Which one are we supposed to take?"

He bent over Carmela, brushing her hair from her face. Carlisle's roar of rage came from nowhere as he lunged at the man, tackling him to the ground. They struggled, fists flying, and the second man rushed toward them.

I crawled to Carmela, my hands shaking as I pressed them against her neck, feeling for a pulse. "Carm, please..." My voice was a broken whisper, my body racked with sobs. "Please wake up."

A gunshot rang out, the sound shattering the air like a thunderclap. My heart stopped, my breath caught in my throat as time seemed to slow, everything around me narrowing to that single, deafening crack. I jerked, my body reacting instinctively to the violence, and my eyes snapped up, terror seizing me as I saw Carlisle crumple to the ground.

"No," I whispered, the word a broken sob as I watched him fall. It was like something out of a nightmare, his body folding in on itself, collapsing with a heavy, sickening finality. His eyes, once sharp and vibrant, stared blankly up at the sky, lifeless and unseeing, and blood—so much blood—poured from the wound in his chest, pooling beneath him, staining the pavement crimson.

"Carlisle!" I screamed, the sound tearing from my throat, raw and broken, as I reached out toward him. But he didn't move, didn't respond. His body lay there, still and lifeless.

The man standing over him turned to me, his gun still smoking, his eyes cold and unfeeling. He looked at Carlisle's lifeless form, then back at me, his expression a mask of detached indifference, as if he'd just swatted a fly rather than taken a man's life. "Grab her," he barked, his voice harsh and final. "Let's go."

"You bastard," I spat, my voice shaking with fury, with grief. I screamed, dragging myself toward them, but the man closest to me kicked me in the stomach, pain exploding through me as he grabbed Carmela off the ground. "Don't take her… please."

But they ignored me, scooping Carmela's limp form into their arms like she was a doll, her head lolling lifelessly against the man's shoulder. I could barely see through the haze of pain and tears, but I could hear their voices, the urgency in them as they loaded her into the waiting car.

The sound of sirens filled the air, growing louder, but they were too far away, too late. The car sped off as my body crumpled to the ground, every nerve ablaze with pain, each breath a struggle. Carlisle lay just a few feet away, his body twisted at an unnatural angle, eyes staring blankly at the sky as if seeking solace in the clouds that had gathered above. There was no spark of life left in those eyes, only the chilling emptiness of death. My heart ached with a grief so profound it felt like it might shatter into a thousand irreparable pieces.

"No," I whimpered, my voice barely a whisper against the chaos that surrounded us. Blood roared in my ears, and I fought to keep my vision from blurring. My hand trembled as I reached out, desperate to touch him, to somehow bring him back, to feel the warmth of his skin under my fingertips instead of the cold, life-less flesh that greeted me. My fingers brushed against the fabric of his shirt, and the feeble contact sent a wave of anguish crashing over me. He had been so full of life, always infuriatingly cocky, always pushing buttons and boundaries. I had been so angry at him for how he'd treated Carmela—something I could never take back. Now he was still, silent, his life extinguished in an instant.

The muscles in my belly seized, a sharp, stabbing pain radiating through me. I gasped. The breath was stolen from my lungs as I felt the warm, sticky gush between my legs. Panic and fear tangled with the physical agony, twisting through me like barbed wire. *No, no, not my baby. Not now. Please, God, not now.*

The realization came crashing down on me like a massive wave, overwhelming and suffocating; my daughter was dying. My little girl, who I hadn't even held yet, who I had whispered promises to in the quiet hours of the night, who I had dreamed of holding and loving—she was slipping away. My vision blurred with tears, the edges of the world dissolving into a haze of despair.

I turned my head back to Carlisle, the pain in my body paling in comparison to the torment in my heart. He had thrown himself between us and the bullet, his last act one of selfless, reckless bravery. He'd given his life to protect us, to give me, Carmela, and my daughter a chance, and I was failing him. Failing them both.

"Carlisle…" I choked out his name, a sob wrenching from my chest, my voice a broken plea against the finality that had already claimed him. I wanted to tell him how sorry I was for being mad at him, how I wished things had been different. But there were no words strong enough, no words that could convey the magnitude of my regret. The pain in my belly intensified with each passing second, each heartbeat a brutal reminder of time as it seemed to slip away.

The darkness edged closer, creeping in from the corners of my vision, but I fought it, clawed against it, desperate to hold on. *Please, don't take her from me. I'm so sorry.* The words were a mantra, a desperate prayer to the universe, to anyone who would listen. *Let me keep her. I'm so sorry, Carlisle. For everything.*

The agony surged, white-hot and unrelenting, and I knew I was losing her. My baby girl, the only link I had to Beckett was slipping away, and I couldn't stop it. I was supposed to protect her, to keep her safe, but I was failing, and the guilt was a crushing weight, suffocating me. *I'm so sorry, little one. I'm so, so sorry.*

My body trembled, the strength bleeding from me, the fight slipping through my fingers like sand. I let my eyes close, the world fading to black, my heart breaking as I surrendered to the darkness. *I can't do this. I can't lose you both. Please, let me go too.*

The last thought, the final desperate wish, slipped from my mind like a whisper, like a sigh. *I'm so sorry. Let me die, too.*

And then there was nothing but silence, a cold, empty void where there had once been pain.

six

BECKETT

LIFE WAS FILLED with decisions that haunt you, each one leaving an indelible mark. For me, the one that clawed at my soul, that haunted my every waking moment, was the decision to walk away from Celestina, to leave her with Tino nearly ten months ago. Every sleepless night was plagued by the memory of her terrified expression as I shoved her into that panic room, her eyes wide with fear and betrayal, her lips trembling as she whispered my name. I'd never forget that look, the way she reached for me even as I forced the door shut between us. That image would be burned into my mind until the day I died.

I'd hoped that time and distance would erase her from my thoughts, that I could somehow push her out of my heart. But it was impossible. She'd carved herself so deeply into my soul that she'd become a part of me. Even as I tried to move on, to bury myself in the violence and chaos that was my life, she was always there, lingering like a ghost at the edges of my mind, her presence haunting me with every breath I took.

61

I'd kept my promise to stay away, even though every fiber of my being screamed to go back to her, to hold her, to tell her I was sorry. After I healed from the gunshot wound—thanks to Tino and his sister—I made a single call, desperate for news.

"Why are you calling me, Mr. Heart?" Massimo Anastasi's voice had been a low growl on the other end of the line, the anger and disdain barely contained.

I inhaled deeply, preparing myself for the conversation I knew was coming. "I need to know she's safe."

The silence that followed was deafening, a heavy, suffocating void that threatened to crush me. His disapproval was almost palpable through the phone, a cold, sharp blade cutting into my chest. I didn't deserve an answer. Hell, I was the reason she'd been taken and put in danger in the first place.

"She's safe." His response was clipped, cold. A single statement that carried a world of meaning. He was telling me to back off, to stay away. "You need to forget about my sister, Mr. Heart."

"I'll never forget her," I snapped, my voice breaking with the anger and regret that bled into every word. I wanted to scream, to rage against the distance, the separation that was tearing me apart. "But I'll stay away. I won't bring death to her doorstep as long as you can protect her until I take care of the threat."

"We are working to end Manuel. You needn't worry about that."

"Oh, I'm not worried, Mr. Anastasi. I'm pissed. He made the mistake of hiring me to do something I rarely do."

"Kidnap women?" There was a bitter laugh coming from the opposite side of the call, a sound that scraped against my raw nerves like broken glass. "And yet you did."

"I'll regret what I did to Celestina for the rest of my life." The confession was torn from me, harsh and jagged, each word a blade slicing into my own heart. "Your sister is a force of nature. She burned herself into my veins. I'll do everything I can to protect her. No one will touch her."

"You love my sister," Massimo said, his tone shifting, as if he were weighing the truth of my words. "Then why stay away? Why not come and help us take him down?"

"I'm death and destruction," I whispered, the truth of it settling heavy in my chest. "She deserves someone who can give her things I cannot."

"You underestimate my sister, Mr. Heart. Celestina is strong, and she has Anastasi blood in her veins. She doesn't want soft, I assure you."

"Your sister deserves a hero."

"Yet she fell in love with a monster." Massimo's voice was resigned, almost sad, the resignation of a man who knew there was no changing what was already written in the stars. "What do I tell her when she asks about you?"

"Tell her to forget me."

"And when she learns where you are… What then?"

"Don't tell her, Mr. Anastasi. I can't be the man she needs."

"Maybe not, but you're the man she wants. Fine," he said, his voice heavy with frustration, the weight of everything we'd lost pressing down on him as much as it did on me. "I'll keep your location secret, but you know as well as I do, secrets never stay buried."

His words echoed in my mind as I stood over the man tied to the chair facing me. The room was cold, the smell of blood and fear hanging thick in the air. The motherfucker groaned, his head slumped forward, blood dribbling from his mouth. I gripped his hair, yanking his head back, and pressed the blade against his throat, my voice low and lethal.

"Tell me where Manuel is hiding."

"Fuck you," he spat, his words slurred through broken teeth, blood pouring down his face, mixing with the dirt and sweat that coated his skin. His eyes burned with defiance, a flicker of something resembling courage in their depths.

I shook my head slowly, a grim smile spreading across my face, the cold edge of my rage slipping into my voice. "You'll die either way, but it can be quick… or not. I was trained to interrogate the enemy, and you, my friend, are the enemy." I leaned in closer, the knife just piercing the delicate skin of his throat. "Did you know if I put just the right amount of pressure here—"I pressed the blade in a little more, his eyes widening with fear. "I can take your head clean off?"

His breath hitched, and he trembled under my grip, his body shaking with the effort to stay calm. "Doesn't matter. I'm not the only one hunting her. Kill me, and someone else will get to her and finish what he started."

His words sent a jolt of fear and fury through me, a lethal cocktail of emotions that set my blood boiling. "What are you talking about?"

An evil grin spread across his battered face, his eyes gleaming with a sick satisfaction, the kind of pleasure that came from watching someone else's world fall apart. "You don't know, do you?"

"Know what?" I growled, pressing my knee into his groin, making him squirm in pain. The knife burrowed deeper into his neck, a thin line of blood trickling down, but he didn't flinch, his smile widening.

"They've gone after your girl several times now. She's a slippery little bitch though. But the last time they made a go at her, they did some real damage."

"What the fuck are you talking about?" I snarled, the rage boiling inside me, the desperation clawing at my chest. "What did they do to her? You said they did some real damage last time. What. Does. That. Mean?"

"Fuck you," he sneered, his voice a ragged whisper, his eyes taunting me with their dark, twisted amusement.

The red haze of rage descended, and I let it consume me. I didn't stop until his head rolled off his shoulders and hit the floor with a sickening thud, his blood splattering across my face, my hands, but I barely noticed. I kicked the chair back, the body slumping to the ground in a grotesque heap. The shack reeked of death and fear, the only sound my labored breathing.

I pulled my phone from my pocket, my fingers shaking as I dialed a number I'd sworn never to use again.

"I don't have time to deal with you, Mr. Heart." Massimo's voice was icy, each word dripping with barely restrained fury.

"I'm busy planning a funeral. One that you brought to this family."

His words hit me like a punch to the gut. My heart stopped, the room spinning as I struggled to breathe. The line went dead, the silence screaming in my ears. I sank to the ground on my knees, The pain was unbearable, a searing, burning agony that ripped through me, leaving me gasping for air, my body trembling with the force of it.

I'd seen men die, had killed more than my share, but nothing had prepared me for the pain ripping through my chest. I stood, wiping the blood from my face with a trembling hand. Manuel might be a monster, but I was something far worse.

I thought of Celestina, of what I'd sacrificed by staying away. Manuel was so focused on the Anastasis, he never considered the man who would destroy him—me. I grabbed a can of accelerant and poured it over the shack's floor, the liquid splashing onto the walls, the smell of gasoline filling the air. I struck a match, the tiny flame flickering in the darkness, and tossed it onto the floor.

The fire caught instantly, roaring to life, the heat scorching my face as I watched the building go up in flames. I stood in the tree line, watching the orange glow devour everything, the smoke curling into the sky like the dark tendrils of my rage. The fire consumed the evidence of my wrath, the ashes of my sins rising into the night, a silent testimony to the destruction I'd wrought.

When there was nothing left but embers, the smoke and ash curling into the night like ghosts of all the lives I'd taken, I turned away, the charred remains of my vengeance smoldering behind me. I hiked my bag onto my shoulder, the weight of it a cruel reminder of what lay ahead. There was only one place left to go, one final stop before I disappeared forever. Manuel might have struck the Anastasis with a deadly blow, but I would annihilate him and his entire organization.

A soldier with nothing left to lose is dangerous. But a man whose heart has been ripped out is nothing but carnage.

I reached my car, the engine's low rumble a stark contrast to the storm raging inside me. Slumping into the driver's seat, I let my head fall against the steering wheel, the cool leather pressing against my forehead. I took a deep breath, the air thick and heavy, the weight of everything pressing on me like an avalanche. I'd fought so hard to protect her, to keep the darkness from touching her, and in the end, I'd failed. Celestina was gone, and I'd failed her in the worst possible way.

But there was still one thing I could do. My last act of redemption, my final offering to the universe that had taken everything from me. I would tear Manuel's world apart, piece by bloody piece, until there was nothing left but ash and ruin.

I pulled into a run-down motel on the outskirts of town, a place that reeked of desperation and despair. The neon sign flickered overhead, casting a sickly glow over the parking lot. The clerk barely glanced at me as I paid for a room in cash, his eyes glazed over with the disinterest of someone who had seen too many broken men, too many haunted eyes. Men like me, running from something, or heading toward destruction.

The room was a dingy, musty mess, the smell of stale cigarettes and mildew hanging in the air like a shroud. The wallpaper peeled in the corners, and the carpet was stained with God knows what. But I didn't care. The state of the room was the least of my concerns. I stripped off my blood-soaked clothes, tossing them into a heap on the floor, and stepped into the bathroom. The mirror was cracked, my reflection fragmented and distorted, a fitting image of the man I'd become.

I turned the water on, the pipes groaning in protest, and stepped under the cold spray. The icy water bit into my skin, washing away the grime and blood, but it couldn't touch the filth that clung to my soul. I scrubbed at my skin, the soap lathering under my hands, turning pink as it mixed with the blood that still lingered. I watched it swirl down the drain, wishing I could wash away the memories as easily.

But there was no escaping them. The ghosts of the past clung to me, whispering accusations, reminding me of every life I'd destroyed, every promise I'd broken.

I thought of Celestina, of the way her eyes had looked when I'd left her. I'd convinced myself I was doing the right thing, that staying away would protect her, would keep her safe. But I'd been a fool. The look on her face, the pain and confusion in her eyes as I'd pushed her away, would haunt me for the rest of my days.

I turned off the water, the cold seeping into my bones, and stepped out of the shower. Grabbing a thin, threadbare towel, I dried off, my skin prickling with the chill. I glanced at the mirror again, at the man staring back at me, his eyes hollow, his face drawn and pale. I barely recognized him. The scars that lined my body were nothing compared to the ones that marred my soul.

I collapsed onto the bed, the mattress lumpy, the pillow scratchy and thin. It didn't matter. I was too exhausted to care. My body ached with a bone-deep weariness, my mind frayed and unraveling at the edges. I had a few hours to rest before I made my way back to Mexico. Before I faced the ghosts that waited for me. Before I said goodbye to the only woman I'd ever love. And before I made good on my promise to destroy anyone who had dared to hurt her.

I closed my eyes, the darkness pulling me under, but it wasn't the peaceful oblivion I craved. Images flickered behind my eyelids, memories and dreams tangled together in a cruel, mocking dance. I saw her, Celestina, her face soft and smiling, the way she used to look at me before everything fell apart. I saw a future that would never be—her laughter filling the air, the feel of her hand in mine, the warmth of her body beside me in the night. I saw a life where I wasn't the monster who'd shattered her heart, where I was worthy of her love, her trust.

But monsters don't get happy endings.

The images twisted, darkened, her smile fading, replaced by the terror and pain I'd seen the last time I'd looked into her eyes. The dreams turned to nightmares, the ghosts of my past clawing at me, dragging me down into the abyss. I saw the faces of the men I'd killed, their eyes accusing, their voices whispering words of condemnation, of damnation. I felt the weight of every sin I'd committed, every life I'd taken, bearing down on me like a vise, squeezing the breath from my lungs.

The darkness was suffocating, the weight of my regrets, my failures, crushing me. I let myself sink into it, let it swallow me whole. Because in that filthy, forgotten room, in the silence and the shadows, there was nothing left for me but the truth I'd been running from all my life.

I was a monster, a destroyer, a harbinger of death. And that's all I would ever be.

CELESTINA

THREE HUNDRED SIXTY-FIVE DAYS, *seven hours, and twenty-three minutes.*

One year ago, I couldn't have told you I'd be staring down at a tiny, wriggling human being—but here I was. And I was damn glad for it. I'd nearly lost my daughter because I'd been stupid enough to want to leave the safety of my house despite knowing full well I was a walking target. The memory of that day played over and over in my head like a broken record, a nightmare that haunted me even when I was wide awake.

The pain was indescribable, unlike anything I'd ever felt, and as the haze slowly cleared from my mind, I tried to blink open my heavy eyelids. The harsh fluorescent lights overhead were like staring directly into the sun, making me squint and turn my head away. The ceiling tiles swam in and out of focus as I struggled to make sense of where I was.

"Hey," a voice broke through the fog, familiar and comforting. I tried to turn my head toward the sound, but it felt like it weighed a thousand pounds. "Whoa, Cee. Take it easy, honey. You're in the hospital."

Harley's face swam into view, her eyes filled with concern as she leaned over me. Drew Mancini's wife, Catarina's best friend…a lifeline in the chaos. "I've called for the doctor, sweetheart. You were in an accident. Do you remember?"

The memories crashed into me like a tidal wave—Carlisle, the car, the fear and pain that felt like it would split me in half. A sob escaped my lips before I could hold it back. "Carmela?" My voice was a fragile whisper, the word catching in my throat.

"Let's wait for the doctor before we talk, okay?" Harley's voice was soft but firm, a gentle plea for me to hold on, to wait.

My hand moved instinctively to my stomach, my heart plummeting when I felt the flatness beneath my palm. The once-round bump, my constant companion for the past nine months, was gone. Panic gripped me, squeezing my chest so tightly I could barely breathe.

"My daughter?" The words were barely a breath, a desperate plea.

"She's in the NICU as a precaution," Harley said gently, her hand covering mine. "You were hurt pretty badly, sweetheart."

The door to my room swung open, and in rushed a whirlwind of bodies—Massimo, Antonio, Vincenzo, and the rest of my family. Massimo was at my side in an instant, his arms pulling me into a gentle embrace, his familiar scent wrapping around me like a safety net.

"Cee… fuck, we thought we lost you."

"I'm sorry," I whispered, my voice breaking.

"None of that," he said quietly, his voice a gentle murmur against my hair. "I shouldn't have kept you locked up…you wouldn't have snuck out."

I cried against his chest. The tears were hot and bitter. "Carlisle…he's dead." The memory of his body hitting the ground played on a loop in my mind. "Oh, fuck. Carmela… where's—"

Massimo pressed a finger to my lips, his eyes filled with anguish. "It's going to be okay, Cee. We'll find her."

"No." I jerked away from him, my hands gripping his shirt. "No, they took her. They took her because of me, Massimo. She's dead because of me. I killed her…I killed my sister."

The doctor rushed in, pushing past my brothers, who stood like a protective wall around my bed. "She's getting too upset," he said sharply, his hands moving quickly as he injected something into my IV. The world blurred, the voices around me fading as the sedative pulled me under—but not before the memory of what I'd done echoed in my mind, a ghost that would never leave me.

NOW, A YEAR LATER, I STOOD OVER THE TINY BASSINET, looking down at my daughter. Emilia's small, perfect face was scrunched up in sleep, the dark wisps of hair on her head soft under my fingertips. She had the Anastasi coloring, but her eyes—those cerulean blue eyes—were all Beckett's. Every time she looked at me, it was like being hit with a sledgehammer, a painful reminder of the man who had given her to me and then disappeared.

The doctor had told me her eyes might change, but I knew they wouldn't. They were Beckett's, just as she was a part of him, a part I couldn't let go of no matter how hard I tried.

Memories of him washed over me, unbidden and unrelenting.

"Tino." Beckett's voice was low, almost hesitant, as if he were unsure of himself. "I have a problem and need your help."

I'd been eavesdropping on him, my anger and confusion fueling my curiosity. I hated him for what he'd done, for the danger he put my family through, but there had been moments…moments when I thought I saw something more in him, something good. And then he said the words that changed everything.

"I'm breaking the contract with Manuel Costa."

My heart had stuttered in my chest. For a moment, I thought I'd misheard him. He was risking everything—for me. I pressed my ear closer to the door, barely breathing.

"A woman," he continued, his voice rough. "It's too bad she's using me because I'm pretty sure she fucking hates me."

Did I? I didn't know. I thought I hated him, but now, as I stood on the other side of that door, my heart felt like it was being squeezed in a vise. I pushed the door open, and his eyes met mine, surprise flickering across his face.

"He was going to make it look like someone from the Bianchi family killed Celestina Anastasi. You know her brothers wouldn't stop until they saw every Bianchi dead."

I walked toward him, my legs trembling. He turned his back to me, continuing his conversation as if I wasn't there. I dropped to my knees, unbuttoning his pants, and he stiffened, his eyes darkening with confusion and lust.

"Yes," Beckett said into the phone, his voice hitching as I wrapped my lips around him. "She's the woman I went against him for."

I didn't hate him. I knew that now. As I pleasured him, I felt something inside me break, something I couldn't put back together. He was in danger because of me, and yet I was here, on my knees, trying to hold onto something that wasn't mine to keep.

He ended the call, tossing the phone aside, his hands tangling in my hair as he lifted me to my feet. The desperation in his eyes matched my own as he laid me down on the table, thrusting into me with a ferocity that left me breathless. I clung to him, my body arching under his, the intensity of our connection searing through me.

"That was a naughty thing to do," he murmured against my skin, his voice thick with desire. "Did you like having my cock fill you like that?"

"God, yes," I gasped, my hands clutching his shoulders as he drove into me, each thrust pushing me closer to the edge.

"I'm sorry I can't be the man for you," he whispered, his words a cruel echo of the pain I'd tried to ignore.

"You could be," I said, my voice breaking, the tears I'd held back finally spilling over. "You could be."

"No, Celestina...I..." He shook his head, his eyes closing as if to shut me out. "Please, just stay here. Don't open the door

or turn on the lights. I'll come for you when it's safe. I promise."

But he hadn't come back. He vanished, and I'd been left with nothing but a shattered heart and a tiny, fragile life I wasn't sure I was strong enough to protect.

Emilia's tiny cry pulled me back to the present. I lifted her from the bassinet, her weight a comforting presence against my chest. She was my lifeline, the reason I hadn't completely crumbled under the weight of my guilt and grief.

"How's my favorite niece?" Vincenzo's voice was soft as he stepped into the room, his smile gentle as he looked at Emilia. "And my favorite sister?"

"Since when am I your favorite?" I asked, my voice thick with emotion. "And she's your only niece."

"Still my favorite." He reached out, taking Emilia from my arms and cradling her against his chest. My heart twisted as I watched him with her, the love and protectiveness in his eyes so fierce it took my breath away. "Becks, anything your momma tells you is all lies."

"Stop calling her that. Her name is Emilia."

"Nope… sorry. You're the one who decided to give her the middle name. She's too tough to be an Emmy—so Becks it is."

I rubbed my forehead, exhaustion pulling at me. "It was the only thing I could give her that was her dad's since you still won't tell me where he is."

Vin's face tightened, the warmth in his eyes replaced with steely resolve. "Until we know where Manuel is, we need to keep her hidden. She's an easy mark, Celestina. And right now, we need to shield her from Manuel's men."

"I get it, Vin. I do."

And I did. Massimo had explained it over and over—we had to keep her safe, to keep her hidden.

And I did. Massimo had explained it to me until he was blue in the face—we had to keep her hidden. My gut churned with disgust at the thought of my sister being missing or worse, dead, and that my daughter was still in danger, anyway. Two long months and my brothers were no closer to finding her. Manuel had made no move to use her, which made everything worse.

Massimo had learned that Manuel Costa was involved with the skin trade business. My worst fears initially were that he'd killed her, but now…I worried he'd sold her. I wasn't sure which was worse—death or the torture she'd be enduring if she was still alive.

"Any word on Carmela?"

"No." Vin shook his head, his eyes darkening at the mention of my sister. "We'll find her, Cee. I promise you."

Beckett's words filtered back in. *I'll come for you when it's safe. I promise.* "I don't believe in promises, Vin."

eight

CELESTINA

THE MAHOGANY WOOD felt oddly cool under my arm as I leaned against it, cradling my two-month-old daughter in the crook of my elbow. She was my lifeline, the only reason I hadn't been completely swallowed by the darkness that constantly threatened to consume me. Glancing up, I saw the other reminder of how my reckless actions had cost us so much—Carlisle's absence hung heavy in the air, an unspoken ache that reverberated through the family, especially Massimo. They had been more than colleagues; they were confidants, brothers in all but blood. The void he left was a stark reminder of the devastation I had brought upon us.

A tear slid down my cheek as I tried to shake off the suffocating guilt pooling in my stomach. My daughter needed a mother who was fully present, not the hollow shell I'd been for weeks. Massimo, ever the perceptive one, had recognized the signs of depression and had practically forced me to come here, surrounding me with a protective detail to ensure I was never alone with my spiraling thoughts.

"How you doing?" Madison's voice broke through my reverie as she slipped onto the stool beside me. Her gaze softened when she looked at Emilia. "Look at that sweet thing."

"I owe you an apology." I turned to her, my throat tightening. "We were supposed to be planning your wedding, and I went and fucked it all up."

"Oh, Cee." Madison leaned forward, wrapping me in a gentle hug. "Massimo and I are fine, I promise. The wedding in Italy will happen when it's meant to. When I agreed to be with him, I knew what I was signing up for. He's an important man, and the family needs him right now."

I managed a small smile. "My brother hit the jackpot when he found you."

"I feel the same way. He saved me in more ways than one." She paused, her eyes searching mine. "What about you, though? How are you holding up…really?"

"Honestly?" I took a shaky breath. "Sometimes, the pain is so unbearable I want to crawl under a rock and never come out. My best friend—no, my other half—is gone because of me. I caused this family to lose two people because I was selfish, and that knowledge is like poison, eating away at my soul."

Madison's eyes glistened with unshed tears. "You can't blame yourself for a madman's obsession. Manuel Costa is the one at fault."

"No, but I can blame myself for putting us in his line of fire. If I hadn't snuck out, two people would still be here. Now one is dead, and my sister is missing." My voice cracked, and Emilia stirred, her tiny face scrunching up in discomfort.

"This little girl is the only thing keeping me tethered to this world…and that scares me."

"Why does it scare you?" Madison asked gently.

"Because it's not enough. She deserves a mother who's whole. A mother who isn't using her as a crutch to stay alive. Without her, I would've given up. She holds the only part of my heart that's still beating."

Before Madison could respond, the sound of heavy footsteps echoed from the entrance. Vincenzo stormed in, his face a mask of barely restrained fury. My spine stiffened as I instinctively held Emilia closer.

"What happened, Vin?" Madison's voice was tight with worry. "Is it Donny and Catarina?"

Vincenzo nodded with his jaw clenched. "Their place was attacked. Donny managed to subdue the asshole and get them out. They're safe at Michael's now, but we need to get you two out of here. Massimo and Antonio are handling things at the scene."

My breath caught in my throat. "Are they—"

"They're fine," Vincenzo assured me, his eyes softening briefly. "But we need to move. Now."

I slid off the stool, adjusting Emilia's blanket around her, my hands shaking. The sudden sound of footsteps approaching from the hall made Vincenzo tense, his hand going to the gun at his side. Madison stepped forward, her body serving as a shield between the potential threat and my daughter.

"What the fuck are you doing here?" Vincenzo's voice was a low growl, filled with barely contained violence.

My heart stuttered as the unmistakable voice I thought I'd never hear again filled the space.

"Your family is in danger." Beckett's voice was rough, strained, and it sent a shiver down my spine. I shook my head against Madison's back, my heart hammering wildly in my chest.

"It can't be him," I whispered, tears prickling my eyes. I stepped out from behind Madison, my gaze locking onto the man who had haunted my thoughts every waking moment and in my dreams. His cerulean eyes met mine, and the air seemed to thicken, every heartbeat echoing in my ears.

"You're supposed to be dead," he whispered, his eyes raking over me, his expression torn between relief and disbelief.

"Sorry to disappoint you." I managed, my voice trembling as I rocked Emilia in my arms. The blanket shifted, revealing her to Beckett. His eyes widened, shock and something else —something raw and unguarded—flashed across his face as he stared at the tiny bundle cradled against me.

He stood frozen. His gaze was riveted on our daughter. I took a tentative step forward, breaking free from Madison's protective hold. Vincenzo moved to intercept, but I held up my hand, stopping him.

"Can you two give us a minute?" I asked, my voice steady despite the turmoil churning inside me.

"Cee, I don't—" Vincenzo started, his voice tight with concern.

"Vin," Madison cut him off, a gentle firmness in her tone. "Let's give them some space. He's here to help, right, Beckett?"

Beckett nodded, his eyes never leaving mine. "Five minutes," Madison said, tugging Vincenzo away. "Then we'll do whatever you want, Vin."

I watched them leave, my heart pounding. Turning back to Beckett, I inhaled deeply. "Why are you here, Beckett? Why now?"

He stepped closer, his hand reaching out before it fell to his side. "I thought you were dead."

I swallowed hard, fighting back the tears that threatened to spill. "You left me and never came back."

"I thought I was protecting you, Celestina," he said, his voice raw with regret.

A bitter laugh escaped me. "You were protecting yourself. My family paid the price for your choices. I've lost so much. So, I'll ask again. Why. Are. You. Here?"

"Because the danger is getting worse, and I needed to help your family." His voice cracked as he glanced at Emilia, then back at me. "I thought I'd lost you."

Emilia stirred, her tiny hands reaching out, and Beckett's fingers brushed against hers. "Why didn't you tell me?" he whispered, his eyes glistening with unshed tears.

"Tell you what?" My voice broke. "That you had a daughter? Why would I? I didn't want you to come back out of some sense of duty. We're fine without you. I have my family… What's left of it."

"You were never just a fling, Celestina," he said, his voice fierce as he reached out, his hand hovering near my cheek before he let it drop again. "I was scared of tainting you."

"I'm an Anastasi," I replied, my laugh hollow. "I'm already tainted, Beckett."

"I love you, Celestina."

I snorted, shaking my head. "He took my sister."

His gaze darkened, the murderous rage in his eyes making my blood run cold. "Manuel?"

I nodded, tears blurring my vision. "I convinced Carmela to sneak me out. I couldn't stand being locked up anymore. She's my twin, she understood…she wanted to help. We hadn't gone far when they attacked us. Carlisle was with us. He died because of me."

Beckett stepped forward, his arms reaching for me, but Emilia let out a soft cry, and he froze.

"Was she with you?" His voice was hoarse.

"I went into labor on the side of the road," I whispered, the memory of that night making my body tremble. "If my brothers hadn't gotten there when they did…we'd both be dead."

"Time's up," Vincenzo's voice cut through the air, his tone hard. "We should get them home. There was an attempt on my older sister and her husband today. Everyone's at Michael's now."

"I'm not leaving her." Beckett's voice was steel, his eyes locked on mine. "I made that mistake once. I won't do it again."

Vincenzo stared at him, a tense silence stretching between them before he gave a single nod. "Let's go."

We moved quickly, Beckett's hand hovering near my back as we made our way to the waiting SUV. Drew's eyes widened when he saw Beckett beside me, but he didn't say a word. Beckett lifted Emilia from my arms, pressing his face to her soft hair, his eyes closing as if in prayer.

"You should have her in a seat," he murmured, his voice thick.

"Yeah, probably," I replied, feeling the absurdity of it all. "But this wasn't planned."

He reached out, his fingers brushing against my arm. "Give her to me."

I hesitated, then let him take her. He cradled her gently, pressing his lips to her head as he murmured words I couldn't hear. His body trembled with an emotion that seemed too vast, too overwhelming for him to contain.

"I never thought I could have something like this, Celestina," he whispered, his voice breaking. "My life is a mess of darkness and death. But you…you gave me something beautiful."

I watched, tears slipping down my cheeks as he held our daughter, his face buried against her tiny body. He had walked away from me without a second thought, and now he was back, holding the most precious thing in my life like she was his salvation.

Where did that leave me?

The SUV pulled up to Michael's estate, the long driveway winding through the trees like a path to some secret sanctuary. Antonio stood at the top of the steps, Massimo beside him. Their faces were set in grim lines, their eyes fixed on Beckett as we climbed out of the car.

"This isn't going to be good," I murmured, glancing at Beckett. "My brothers…they're not going to be happy to see you."

"I'll deal with it," he said quietly, his eyes meeting mine. "I'm not leaving, Celestina. Not again."

Massimo's gaze flicked to me, then to Emilia, and finally back to Beckett. His jaw tightened, but he said nothing as he turned and walked inside. Antonio's expression was a storm of emotions as he followed.

With a deep breath, I took Emilia from Beckett's arms, feeling his gaze on me as we followed my brothers inside. The tension in the room was palpable, the air thick with unspoken words and simmering anger. Beckett stood beside me, his presence a solid, unwavering force at my side.

"Just get it over with," he said, his voice steady. "I'm not leaving."

Riley stepped forward, her eyes flashing as she looked from Beckett to my brothers. "You three act like you're perfect. You've all made mistakes. Maybe it's time you stopped fighting and started working together. This family needs to stick together."

Massimo covered his laugh with his hand, but Vin scowled at him as he spoke. "Fuck off, brother."

"As interesting as this is," I carried Emilia over to Madison and placed her in her arms, "I need a minute alone."

BECKETT

I'D FACED down the devil himself and held the fate of countless lives in the palm of my hand. I'd looked through the scope of my rifle, lined up the crosshairs, and pulled the trigger, sentencing men to death without a second thought. I'd walked through hell and back, leaving a trail of bodies and broken dreams in my wake. But none of that scared me. None of it even came close to the fear that gripped me now as I stood at the base of the stairs, watching Celestina cradle our daughter in her arms.

She was so small, barely a wisp of life nestled against her mother's chest, her tiny fists curled into the fabric of Celestina's shirt. My heart pounded in my chest, the sight of them stealing my breath and my resolve. Celestina had given birth without me, fought through the agony and danger alone, while I'd convinced myself that staying away was the right thing to do. That it was safer, better for them both. But as I stood there, rooted to the spot, the weight of my decisions pressed on me like an unbearable, threatening to crush me.

Every nightmare I'd ever had, every doubt and fear I'd buried, paled in comparison to this moment. The woman I loved, the child I never thought I'd have, right there in front of me. And I was paralyzed.

I watched her move up the stairs, her steps slow and deliberate, the exhaustion clear in every line of her body. I wanted to go to her, to tell her I was sorry, that I'd been a coward. I wanted to beg her forgiveness, to hold them both and never let go. But as I took a step forward, a hand settled on my shoulder, halting me.

"Give her a few minutes, Beckett. She's been through hell. We all have."

The voice was gentle but firm, and I turned to find myself face to face with a woman who bore a striking resemblance to Celestina. Her eyes were the same deep, soulful brown, her features etched with a strength and wisdom that spoke of a lifetime of battles fought and scars earned.

"I'm Catarina, her sister." Her voice was calm, though there was an edge to it, a quiet strength that demanded respect. "I'll go check on her. You've got some things to work out down here with my brothers."

I nodded, swallowing hard, the lump in my throat making it difficult to speak. "I—thank you."

Catarina gave me a small, tight smile, her gaze softening just a fraction. "She'll need time, Beckett. And so will you. But she's stronger than you know. Stronger than all of us, maybe."

With that, she turned and ascended the stairs, her steps confident and sure. I watched her go. The sound of her footsteps faded as she disappeared around the corner. My eyes drifted back to the spot where Celestina had stood, the emptiness there a stark reminder of the distance I'd created between us.

I took a deep breath, trying to steady myself, but the fear, the guilt, the regret—they were a storm raging inside me, threatening to tear me apart. I believed I was safeguarding them by staying away, by maintaining my distance. But I'd been a fool. A coward. I'd let my fear control me, let it drive me to make decisions that I now knew had been all wrong.

Reluctantly, I let go of my need to chase after Celestina and turned to face the room full of Anastasis. Massimo gestured toward the living room with an unreadable expression.

"Mr. Heart."

The voice was low, familiar, and I turned to see Massimo standing in the doorway, his expression unreadable. Behind him, Donny and Drew lingered, their faces grim. They were a wall of silent judgment, brothers who had stood by Celestina when I hadn't, who had watched over her and our daughter while I'd hidden behind my fears.

"We need to talk," Massimo said, his tone brooking no argument. His eyes were dark, intense, as he watched me with a wariness I'd never seen before. This was a man who'd faced down enemies, made life and death decisions, and yet, right now, I was the one in the crosshairs.

"I don't plan to give Celestina a lot of time to stew." My voice was calm, but my nerves were a live wire under the surface, buzzing with anxiety and regret. I moved toward Madison, who stood next to Massimo, cradling my daughter in her arms. My daughter. The thought still floored me, knocked the breath out of me every time it hit.

"Please, give me my daughter," I said, holding out my hands.

Madison hesitated, her eyes searching mine, as if trying to decide whether to trust me with the precious little life she held. Then, with a small nod, she carefully placed Emilia in my arms. As soon as I felt the warmth of her tiny body against my chest, the world seemed to right itself. My heartbeat steadied, the storm inside me calming. This little girl was a miracle, a piece of Celestina and me, a life I'd never thought I'd be blessed with. I was going to fight like hell to keep her—and her mother—safe.

Massimo settled onto the couch, pulling Madison onto his lap, his gaze never leaving me. He was a fortress of strength and protectiveness, his posture relaxed but alert, ready to spring into action at the slightest hint of threat. "I'm assuming your presence here wasn't because you came back for her. So, tell me, Mr. Heart… why are you here?"

"Call me Beckett," I corrected, holding Emilia closer, her tiny weight grounding me. "And you're wrong. I am here for her. I fucked up by leaving because I thought it would keep her safe. Clearly, I was wrong."

"Clearly," snapped the youngest of the brothers, Antonio. His eyes were hard, his jaw clenched tight with anger that radiated off him in waves. "She was nearly killed. Our sister is gone, probably dead. You were supposed to keep her safe, and you failed. So yeah, I'd say you were wrong."

"Antonio." Massimo's voice was low, a warning that seemed to vibrate through the room. "Not helping."

Antonio threw his hands up in mock surrender, but his eyes were still burning with a fury that made my chest tighten.

"Fine," he muttered, but the bitterness in his voice lingered, hanging in the air like smoke.

I was about to respond, to try and explain, when a man stepped up behind Antonio, wrapping his arms around his waist in a gentle, grounding embrace. He leaned in close, whispering something into Antonio's ear that I couldn't hear, but it was like watching a flame being doused. The anger drained from Antonio's face, his shoulders relaxing as he leaned back into the man's hold. The intimacy of the moment, the way Antonio's face softened, caught me off guard, and I looked away, feeling like an intruder in their private moment.

Emilia fussed in my arms, her tiny face scrunching up as if she could sense the tension in the room. I rocked her gently, my hand cradling the back of her head, the other resting on her small, warm back. The soothing motion seemed to calm her, her soft whimpers fading into quiet, steady breaths. I glanced down at her, marveling at the fragility and strength wrapped up in this small, perfect being. How had I thought I could protect her and Celestina by staying away?

"I know I fucked up," I said. My voice was low but steady as I looked up at Massimo, meeting his hard, unwavering gaze. "I thought I was protecting them by keeping my distance, but I was wrong. I should have been here. I should have fought beside her, not from the shadows."

The silence that followed was thick and suffocating, the weight of my confession hanging in the air. Every pair of eyes in the room bore into me, each gaze carrying its own judgment, its own pain. I felt exposed, raw, every word I'd spoken a wound laid bare for them all to see.

"Let me take her," Catarina said softly, stepping forward, her hand outstretched. "She might need a diaper change."

I hesitated, my arms tightening instinctively around my daughter. Emilia squirmed slightly, her small face contorting as if she had gas. Reluctantly, I handed her over, watching as Catarina cradled her with a tenderness that both soothed and ached. I felt a pang of loss as she carried Emilia away, the room suddenly feeling too empty, too vast without the small, comforting presence of my child.

Turning back to the men in the room, I squared my shoulders, facing their scrutiny head-on. They had every right to hate me, to question my intentions. I'd left Celestina when she needed me most, and nothing I could say would erase that.

"I found out that Manuel was still targeting Celestina, even though I did everything I could to lead him away," I began, my voice steady but laced with the frustration and guilt that had been eating at me for months. "But I was too late. I have a lead on where he might be, and once I know she's safe, I'm going after him."

Massimo's eyes narrowed, his jaw tightening. "You think that's wise? Leaving her again for revenge? Vengeance gets you nothing, Beckett. You'll be risking the woman you love. And I assume you do love her."

"I do," I replied without hesitation, meeting his gaze head-on. "But I need to know she's safe. I need to know they're both safe." I glanced at the door Catarina had disappeared through, feeling the familiar ache of longing in my chest. "Now more than ever."

Massimo's gaze softened slightly, the harsh lines of his face easing, but his voice remained firm. "We'll make sure of that.

But you need to fix things with Celestina. If she doesn't want you here, you won't be welcome. Daughter or not."

"I'll do whatever it takes," I vowed, the desperation in my voice echoing in the quiet room.

"Then go upstairs and make it right." He nodded toward the stairs, his eyes locking onto mine. "Her room is the second one on the left."

I didn't need to be told twice. I stood, my legs trembling slightly as I crossed the room. My heart raced in my chest, Reaching her door, I paused, my hand hovering over the door-knob. I drew a deep breath, then turned it and stepped inside.

The room was dimly lit, the soft glow of a bedside lamp casting long, shifting shadows on the walls. Celestina stood by the window, her back to me, shoulders tense, her silhouette framed against the night sky. The sight of her, so close yet so far, made my heart ache with a fierce, almost unbearable longing.

"For three months, I prayed you'd come find me," she said in a soft but edged voice with a raw, aching pain that sliced through me. "Days turned into weeks, then weeks into months. And you never came."

Her words hung in the air, heavy and accusing, each one a dagger aimed straight at my heart. I opened my mouth to respond, but she continued, her voice trembling with the weight of her confession.

"I was so sick. I thought it was because my heart was broken. But then I saw the positive sign, and I realized… I was pregnant. At first, I was angry. You'd left, and now I was stuck with this constant reminder that you'd been mine, even if only for a short time. But then I understood something."

She turned, her eyes locking onto mine, and the anguish in them shattered something deep inside me.

"I prayed for you, Beckett. I prayed for something to prove that what I felt for you was real. And I got her. Emilia is the love I thought I'd never get to have with you. She's the reason I'm still here, still fighting. Because when I woke up in that hospital, when they told me I'd lost my sister and had an emergency C-section...I wanted to die."

My breath hitched at her words, my chest constricting painfully. "Celestina…"

"I died inside that day, Beckett. And then they laid her on my chest, and I knew I had to keep fighting. Not for me, but for her." She took a deep breath, her eyes glassy with unshed tears. "I'm so empty inside, Beckett. I'm a shell of who I was. Our daughter deserves more than that. But I don't know if I can ever get back to who I was."

I took a step forward, my hands aching to reach out and hold her, to bridge the chasm between us. "I'm going to find your sister, Celestina. I promise you."

She laughed, a bitter, hollow sound that sent a shiver down my spine. "Funny thing about promises, Beckett. They're just words people say to make themselves feel better. They don't mean a damn thing."

"I know I failed you before. I know that." I reached out, cupping her cheek gently, and was surprised when she didn't pull away. Her skin was warm and soft under my palm, the touch grounding me, anchoring me in a way I hadn't felt in months. "But leaving you was the hardest thing I've ever done. You took this—" I took her hand and pressed it against my chest, right over my pounding heart. "When I walked away. I know I have to prove myself to you, but I'm not leaving again. Not unless you make me."

Her eyes were wet, filled with a pain and fear that made my heart break. "I can't risk what's left of my heart, Beckett." Her voice trembled as she pushed me back, her hands shaking. "You shattered it into a million pieces. Then I lost my sister, and what was left of it crumbled. The only thing I have left is for her, and I'm scared it won't be enough."

I lifted her chin, forcing her to look at me, my own eyes burning with unshed tears. "I'll leave if that's what you want, Celestina. But not without fighting for you and our daughter. What's her full name?"

She hesitated, then whispered, "Emilia Beckett Heart."

The words struck me like a physical blow, my chest tightening with a mix of love and guilt so intense it was almost suffocating. "You gave her my name."

"I was so angry that you left, but I couldn't let you go. It was the only way I could feel connected to you."

"Jesus, Celestina." I ran a hand through my hair, my voice breaking. "I don't expect you to," I whispered, my voice thick with emotion. "But I'll be here, every day, proving to you that I'm not going anywhere."

"I don't want you to leave your daughter, but I don't know if I can forgive you." Her voice was shaky, the vulnerability in her eyes cutting through me like a knife.

I didn't think. I just moved, stepping forward and threading my fingers through her hair, drawing her lips to mine. She resisted at first, but then, like fire and gasoline, we ignited. The kiss was fierce, desperate, a clash of pain and passion that left me reeling. This woman was everything I wanted, everything I craved, and I knew I would fight to my last breath to keep her.

A knock at the door shattered the fragile moment, breaking us apart. I turned, still breathing hard, to see Catarina standing there, a soft smile on her lips.

"I'm sorry, but she's hungry, and I didn't think you'd want me whipping out my tit to feed her."

Celestina let out a soft, almost embarrassed laugh, wiping at her eyes. "It's all right, Cat." Her voice was steady now, though her eyes were still stormy with emotion. "This is Beckett. Beckett, meet my sister, Catarina."

"We've met." I gave her a small smile, taking Emilia from her arms. She squirmed slightly, her tiny face scrunching up, and I felt a rush of fierce protectiveness wash over me.

I watched, transfixed, as Celestina lifted her shirt and guided our daughter's mouth to her breast. It was such a simple, natural act, but I couldn't look away, couldn't stop the flood of emotions that surged through me. Love, awe, fear, and hope, all tangled together, making my chest ache.

Catarina's soft laugh pulled me from my thoughts. "As entertaining as this is, Massimo wants to speak to you, Beckett."

I nodded, turning back to Celestina, who met my gaze with a mixture of strength and uncertainty. "I'll be back."

I nodded, turning to Celestina. "I'll be back."

We walked downstairs together, my hand resting protectively on Celestina's lower back. I felt like I'd finally found something worth holding on to, and I wasn't about to let it slip through my fingers.

Massimo and the others were waiting in the living room, their expressions tense.

"Let's get this over with," I said, my voice firm. "I have more important things to deal with."

"I hate this," Celestina murmured, drawing everyone's attention. "I've ruined your plans again."

Madison stepped forward, her smile reassuring. "You've done no such thing, Cee. And the big wedding will still happen. It's just going to have to wait a little longer."

"No big deal," Madison shrugged. "We're already married."

The room erupted into chaos. Shouts of surprise and excitement filled the air, the tension breaking like a dam. I watched Celestina and saw the pain flicker across her face as she watched her family celebrate.

I stepped closer, lifting her chin, my heart aching at the vulnerability in her eyes.

"I'm here, Celestina," I whispered. "I'm not leaving. I'll say it as many times as I need to for you to believe me. I want this, with you."

Her tears fell freely, but she didn't look away. "I'm scared, Beckett. So scared."

"Then let's be scared together." I held her gaze, pouring everything I felt into my words. "I want to be here for you, for her. For everything."

She hesitated, then nodded slowly. "Okay. We'll try. But I can't promise anything."

"That's enough for me."

With a deep breath, she handed Emilia to Madison, then took my hand. "Let's go upstairs. We have a lot to talk about."

We walked up the stairs together, side by side, our hands clasped tightly. Whatever the future held, we'd face it together. And I knew, without a doubt, that I would do whatever it took to prove to her that this time, I was never letting go.

ten

CELESTINA

MY DAUGHTER'S soft mewl pulled me from the depths of sleep, a momentary surge of panic tightening in my chest. As I blinked awake, the sight before me stole my breath. Beckett was lying beside me in bed, his bare chest gently rising and falling as he held our daughter against him. The sight was surreal, a vision I'd never dared to dream would be real. He looked so at peace, his arm wrapped securely around Emilia, as if he'd been born to be her protector.

"Are you staring at us?" His voice, deep and rough from sleep, washed over me, drawing the first real smile to my lips in weeks. It wasn't forced, wasn't just for Emilia's sake—it was genuine.

"Where's your shirt?" I teased, arching an eyebrow.

Beckett shifted carefully, rolling to his side and placing Emilia between us. He brushed his fingers over a tiny black curl on her head and grinned, the kind of smile that made my heart ache in the best way.

"She was restless, and I wanted you to sleep. Your sister suggested skin-to-skin contact to soothe her. Worked like a charm." He chuckled, his gaze softening as he watched our daughter. "Becks fell asleep almost immediately."

"Oh God, not you, too." I groaned, playfully rolling my eyes. "I hate that nickname."

He raised an eyebrow, his grin widening. "I like it." He reached out, his fingers trailing down my cheek, a featherlight touch that sent shivers through me. "You needed the rest, sugar."

"Thank you." I glanced at our daughter, feeling the overwhelming love and responsibility settle back over me. "I need to use the bathroom. Can you put her in the crib? I don't want her to get used to sleeping in our bed."

I hurried to the ensuite, grateful for the brief moment of solitude. As I splashed cool water on my face, I caught a glimpse of myself in the mirror. There was a weariness there, a depth of sorrow I hadn't acknowledged. I took a deep breath, giving myself a quick pep talk before brushing my teeth and heading back into the bedroom.

The sight that greeted me had my heart skipping a beat. Beckett was sprawled out on the bed, his arms stretched over his head, one hand draped lazily across the pillow. His body, sculpted and strong, looked like it belonged to a marble statue, each muscle etched in perfect relief. But my eyes were drawn to the scar near his belly button, a reminder of the day everything changed.

I stepped forward, my fingers drawn to the raised skin. "Is this from that day… from Manuel's men?"

His hand shot out, gripping my wrist gently but firmly, halting my touch. "Celestina… you can't touch me like that."

I snatched my hand back, cradling it to my chest as if I'd been burned. "I'm sorry—"

Before I could finish, Beckett pulled me onto the bed, rolling over me so I was pinned beneath his weight, his face inches from mine. His eyes, dark and intense, burned with something raw and desperate.

"I'm hanging on by a thread, Celestina. Touching me like that…it'll lead to things you're not ready for."

I closed my eyes, the conflict inside me a storm I couldn't control. "I'm not the same woman you remember, Beckett. My body…it's not the same."

His hands framed my face, forcing me to look at him. "Look at me, Celestina." His voice was rough, almost pleading. "Nothing—absolutely nothing—about you will ever make me want you less. Having our baby only makes me want you more."

A tear slipped down my cheek, a tiny release of the torrent of emotions trapped inside me. "The accident… I was unconscious by the time they found me. I'd been in labor for a while, and when I got to the ER, the doctor had to do an emergency C-section. It…it scarred me, Beckett. It left my body in pieces."

He leaned down, his thumb swiping at the tear. "I want to trust you, but…"

"I know," he whispered, his eyes full of regret and determination. "But I'll earn it back, Celestina. I'll spend the rest of my life earning it back."

He pressed a soft kiss to my forehead before rolling off me. I watched, still caught in the whirlwind of his presence, as he pulled his t-shirt over his head. The way his muscles moved, the strength in his body… it was mesmerizing. He caught my gaze and turned slowly, a playful grin lifting his lips.

"Like what you see?"

I blushed, shaking my head, but I couldn't help the small smile that curved my lips. He came around the bed, holding out his hand.

"Come on. Let's get downstairs. I'm sure everyone's eaten by now, but we can scrounge up something."

I slipped my fingers into his, and he tugged me to my feet. He cupped my cheek, his expression softening as he gazed down at me.

"I'm sorry I hurt you, Celestina. That was never my intent. Even if we never get back to where we were, I'll always protect you and Emilia. I swear it."

As he let go and stepped away, I felt a profound sense of loss, as if something vital had been severed. Grabbing the baby monitor, I checked on our daughter one last time before joining him at the door. He watched me, his eyes never leaving mine as I approached.

I reached out, taking his hand again, lacing our fingers together. "Baby steps," I murmured.

"Baby steps," he echoed, his grin nearly undoing me.

The house was dark and quiet as we made our way downstairs. I wasn't surprised to find Vincenzo sitting at the kitchen table alone, nursing a glass of amber liquor. He looked up as we entered, his expression unreadable.

"I wondered when you'd finally come down. Where's Becks?"

I groaned at the nickname they'd all adopted. "Asleep. I brought the monitor." Setting it down on the counter, I moved to the fridge. "How about a sandwich?"

"That'll do." He glanced at Beckett. His gaze was sharp. "What intel do you have on Manuel's whereabouts?"

Beckett slid into the chair opposite Vincenzo. "You going to go off half-cocked on your own again?"

I turned, meeting Beckett's gaze as he looked at me. "No."

"Good." Vincenzo's eyes narrowed. "Then be ready to sit down tomorrow and work out a plan. There will be others joining us."

"Others?" I stepped forward, my heart pounding. "What others?"

"Father, for one. Now that Mother is safe in Sicily, he'll be joining us on the hunt for Carmela and Manuel."

My heart clenched at the mention of my mother. She hadn't taken the news of Carmela's disappearance well. My father had whisked her away to Italy with my grandmother, hoping to keep her safe. "Does he know Beckett's here?"

"Yep." Vincenzo's smirk told me our father wasn't going to be kind to Beckett.

"And the others?" I pressed, needing to know what we were walking into.

"People who stand to lose just as much if Manuel expands his reach." Vincenzo drained his glass, setting it in the sink. "Tomorrow morning. Ten o'clock."

With that, he left, the room feeling colder in his absence. Beckett turned back to me with a puzzled expression. "Your brother is kinda scary."

A laugh bubbled up, and I had to cover my mouth to stifle it. "Do you not know who my brother is?" He shook his head, his confusion deepening. "Vincenzo isn't just a chef, Beckett. He's one of the deadliest men on the planet. Even though he retired from that side of the family business, he has no problem bringing '*La Lama*' out to play."

Beckett's eyes widened, and he choked on his sandwich, coughing to clear his throat. "Your brother is *La Lama*? Holy shit. It's a miracle I got you out of the bar that night."

His words, though innocent, stung. I tried to hide my reaction, but Beckett saw right through me.

"Shit. I'm sorry, baby."

"It's fine." I took a bite of my sandwich, trying to ignore the pain that had lodged itself in my chest.

Beckett reached across the table, his thumb brushing against my lower lip. "You've got mayo there."

My breath hitched, his touch sending a shiver through me. The air between us crackled with an intensity that made it hard to breathe.

"God, I've missed you," he whispered, his voice breaking. "Say you'll give me a chance, Celestina. Say you can try to love me."

I hesitated. The truth was heavy on my tongue. His eyes were so full of hope, so vulnerable, I couldn't lie to him. "I can't try to love you, Beckett."

Pain flickered in his eyes, and he nodded slowly. "I understand."

Cupping his cheek, I shook my head. "No, you don't. I can't try to love you because I already do."

His breath caught, and the raw emotion in his gaze nearly broke me. "Say it again."

"That day, at your house, I wanted to tell you I was falling for you. But then you shoved me into the safe room, and everything changed." His eyes closed and his expression was pained. "You told me not to get attached. But I had, Beckett. I already had. And I'm still in love with you, even if it breaks me to admit it."

Beckett's gaze locked onto mine, and for a moment, the world faded away. Then, like a dam breaking, he pulled me to him, his lips crashing over mine. It was desperate and fierce, full of the longing we'd both kept buried for so long.

When he finally pulled back, his eyes were dark and intense. "I'll never willingly walk away again." He stood, his hand still holding mine. "Let's try to get some sleep. Tomorrow, we find your sister and put an end to Manuel."

I followed him up the stairs, our fingers intertwined, hope blooming cautiously in my chest. This might be the biggest mistake of my life, but it was one I was willing to make. Because for the first time in a long time, I felt like I was breathing again. And I'd take that risk—if it meant I had a chance at keeping him.

eleven

BECKETT

THE SUNLIGHT FILTERED through the wooden blinds, casting a warm orange glow across the room. It was early, and everything was still and quiet, save for the soft breaths of the two most important people in my life. Celestina lay beside me on her side, her arm tucked under her head as if she'd been searching for something to hold onto in her sleep. Emilia, our tiny miracle, was swaddled snugly against her, a peaceful expression on her face as she dreamed, her tiny fists resting by her cheeks.

Last night, Emilia had woken up crying for a feeding, and I'd watched in awe as Celestina, eyes half-closed but determined, had pulled her to the bed and cradled her close. The sight of Celestina feeding our daughter was something I would never forget. It was pure, raw, and utterly captivating. Love, fierce and all-consuming, had surged through me, locking me in place as I realized just how much these two meant to me.

Gently, I eased Emilia from Celestina's arms, her little mouth still making sucking motions even in her sleep. Her tiny body felt so delicate in my hands, and I moved with the utmost care, carrying her over to the crib. I placed her down carefully, tucking a lightweight blanket over her, and then leaned down to press a soft kiss against her forehead. The scent of her—a blend of milk and baby powder—filled my senses, grounding me in this new reality I never thought I'd have.

Returning to the bed, I laid on my back, staring up at the ceiling. My mind raced with thoughts, worries, and plans for the future, but the steady rhythm of Celestina's breathing calmed the storm inside me. She shifted in her sleep, her body naturally gravitating toward mine as if we were magnets. Her leg draped over my thighs, her arm sliding over my chest. The heat of her breath brushed against my skin, sending a shiver down my spine.

I closed my eyes, fighting a battle I knew I was losing. Every inch of my body reacted to her closeness, the soft press of her curves against me. My hand itched to explore, to trace the lines of her body I knew so well, but I kept still, afraid to disturb her peace. She deserved rest after everything she'd been through, and I was determined to give it to her, even if it killed me.

Her palm rested over my heart, the warmth of her touch seeping into my skin. I reached up, covering her hand with mine, and squeezed gently. It was a simple gesture, but it held everything I couldn't say. All the love, the regret, the promises I was desperate to keep.

At least that's what I thought until her tiny fingers pushed beneath the elastic waistband and wrapped around my shaft. "Celestina," I growled, unsure of what she was doing. "What are you doing?"

She pumped her fist around my shaft, her core pressing into my thigh harder.

"I…" She blew out a breath. "I want you, Beckett."

Like a damn breaking, I pulled her hand out and rolled my body on top of hers, pinning her to the mattress. When my cock ground into her center, she let out a hiss of pleasure. "Are you sure, Celestina? Because I can wait until you're truly ready."

Her response was to grind her hot center against my shaft. "I need to feel something good again. Can you do that for me? Can you make me forget and just… feel?"

I stared down at her. Her bottom lip was caught between her teeth as she waited for my reply. Leaning forward, I covered her mouth with mine, forcing her lips to open. She moaned as I let my tongue explore her mouth, demanding her submission. Shifting my side, I ran my palm up her belly, pushing up the t-shirt she was wearing. I could see the fear in her orbs as I pushed my fingers beneath the elastic of her panties. When my finger found its way into her slick pussy, I groaned.

"Fuck, baby. You're tight. Having my baby didn't change a damn thing about you."

"C-section. Remember?" She turned her head to the side, avoiding my gaze.

"Look at me, baby. I want you to watch as I consume you… see how much I want you… feel what you do to my own body. Having my baby only made you sexier."

I shifted, so I was between her legs. Winding the flimsy satin material around my finger, I jerked, ripping it in two. Tossing the offending fabric to the floor, I pushed her legs further apart. I traced the red scar that ran from hip to hip, making her hiss.

"This is nothing to be ashamed of." I pressed a kiss to the scar, signifying my daughter's entry into the world. "It's a badge of honor."

Kissing my way down her hip, I paused to open her folds. Her sweet musky scent sent bolts of electricity straight to my cock, making it even harder. Pressing my lips to the inside of her thigh, Celestina jerked. My eyes shifted to look up at her and there was trepidation in her expression.

"Do you want me to stop?"

"No, it's just…" She pursed her lips. "What if you don't like how it tastes? Having a baby may've changed things."

Wanting to put those thoughts out of her head, I flicked my tongue out and dragged it through her slick folds. Her intake of breath only spurred me on. I pressed my lips over her folds, sucking the delicate flesh into my mouth. Celestina leaned her head back and moaned into the room as her hips flexed into my face.

"You taste fucking perfect, baby." I dove back in, delving my tongue into the depths of her core. Pushing in a finger, I alternated between sucking her clit and pressing the rough spot inside, the spot I knew would push her over the edge.

"Oh, fuck," She groaned, her body tensing around my digit as I pumped it in and out of her pussy. "Beckett…"

Her orgasm ripped through her like a tsunami leveling a small island in the ocean. Moving up her body, I trailed feather light kisses across her skin. When I reached her face, I slammed my mouth over hers again, claiming her body and soul.

"Are you sure, baby? I don't have to go any further."

"Please, Beckett." Celestina wrapped her legs around my calves and tugged me forward. "I need you inside me."

Needing no further encouragement, I reached between our fused bodies and guided my shaft between her folds. With as much restraint as possible, I slowly buried myself inside her, Celestina's eyes slammed shut, and she made a sound close to a growl when my balls slapped against her ass.

"Look at me, baby. Let me see your eyes when I take you." Her deep brown orbs snapped open as I eased myself nearly all the way out, then slammed back inside. "Fuck… you feel even better than I remembered."

Pressing my lips to hers, I found a rhythm as we moved together. Unlike the times before, this was different. This time, the feelings I tried so hard to ignore were right at the forefront, and I realized walking away from her was the dumbest thing I'd ever done in my life. As her body met mine thrust for thrust, I knew the moment her orgasm hit. Her pussy clenched around my shaft like a vacuum, dotting my vision with black dots. When she cried out my name, I swear I was on the verge of passing out. Her eyes closed again as the pleasure washed over her. The sight of her flushed cheeks toppled me over the edge, and I careened into pure bliss as my cock exploded inside her.

Collapsing over her, I used my elbows as props, keeping my weight off her as I caught my breath. "Fuck." I grunted, finally rolling to my side and flopping onto my back. "Celestina…"

She snuggled against me, pressing her palm against my chest. "I don't remember it being like that."

"No, definitely not." I ran my hand down her side when it hit me. "Shit… I didn't use protection, baby. I'm sorry. I should have been more careful with you."

"It's fine. I'm not due for my period for a while, so we should be ok. I can get the morning-after pill today and take it."

The thought of her being pregnant and ending it didn't sit right with me. "No. Don't do that." I rolled over her again, wedging my body between her legs. "I missed the first baby, Celestina. I won't miss another one. I love you, and I'm going to spend the rest of my life proving that to you. So, let's just leave it to fate, okay?"

Celestina bit down on her lip and nodded slowly. "Okay," she whispered.

"Let's go shower and see who it is that your brothers have invited to go to war with us." I rolled off the bed and stood, holding my hand out to her. "Come on…Let's go get dirty again to get clean."

She giggled as I pulled her to her feet and led her toward the bathroom. Just as we reached the door, Emilia's tiny wail filled the room. Celestina stopped, her eyes drifting to the crib where our daughter was starting to stir.

"I'll get her while you shower," she said softly, though the reluctance in her voice told me she wanted to join me.

"No." I caught her hand, pulling her back toward me. "Bring her with us."

"In the shower?" Her eyes widened in surprise, her brow arching with uncertainty.

"Baby, she's three months old. She won't know or care that we're naked. Bring her along. I want to be with both of you. I want to shower with the two women I love."

Her eyes softened as she looked at me, the hesitance fading. Standing at the entrance to the bathroom, I watched as she hurried over to the crib and scooped Emilia up. Her movements were gentle, filled with that maternal grace that never failed to stir something deep inside me. Celestina carefully stripped our daughter down, discarding her diaper and wiping her clean before lifting her back into her arms.

"Maybe I should feed her first," she suggested, glancing over her shoulder.

"No, bring her in. If she gets hungry, you can feed her in there. I need to be close to you both right now. I need this, Celestina." My voice was a plea, the ache in my chest intensifying as I watched them together.

With a slight nod, she swayed toward me, Emilia cradled securely in her arms. I reached out, placing a soft kiss on Emilia's downy head, inhaling that sweet, innocent baby scent that I'd never get enough of.

"Morning, sweet pea," I whispered, my heart swelling as her tiny face turned toward me, her eyes blinking up with that innocent wonder. "Let's get you cleaned up, yeah?"

I carefully took her from Celestina, cradling her against my chest. The feeling of her small, warm body against mine was overwhelming in the best way. It grounded me, made me feel connected in a way I'd never known was possible.

"Damn," Celestina muttered, a smile tugging at her lips as she watched me. "Seeing you hold her like that… It's a big turn-on and a cock block, all at the same time."

I couldn't help but laugh at the blush coloring her cheeks, my grin widening. "We'll have plenty of time for us. Right now, I just want to enjoy this moment with you two."

She gave me a playful roll of her eyes before turning to step into the bathroom, the sound of the shower filling the room as she turned on the water. Her brother hadn't spared any expense in designing this space. The shower was like a small oasis, spacious and equipped with multiple showerheads that created a cascade of water, more like a gentle rain than a harsh spray.

Emilia's small, restless movements against my chest calmed as the warmth of the room enveloped us. I swayed gently, rocking her in my hold as she stared up at me with wide, curious eyes. She sucked on her tiny fingers, the sound of the water soothing her.

It was such a simple moment yet it felt monumental. This tiny, precious life I was holding—my daughter—was a part of me, a part of us. And Celestina, the woman who'd fought so hard to bring her into this world, was standing there, looking back at me with a softness that made my chest ache.

I stepped into the shower, careful to keep Emilia shielded from the direct spray. Celestina's gaze followed me, a smile playing on her lips as I adjusted the water, letting it cascade over us gently. She reached out, her hand running down Emilia's tiny back, the water droplets clinging to her soft skin.

"I love you," she whispered, her voice barely audible over the sound of the water. It was like a confession, a reminder of everything we'd been through, everything we still had to face.

"I love you, too," I murmured back, my voice thick with emotion. "Both of you. More than I ever thought possible."

We stood there, the water washing over us, cleansing not just our bodies but the lingering shadows of the past year. Celestina leaned in, her lips brushing mine in a kiss that was gentle, tender. It was a promise, a vow that we'd face whatever came our way—together.

Emilia let out a soft coo, her tiny fingers reaching up as if to grasp the air between us. I pressed a kiss to her forehead, feeling the overwhelming surge of love that seemed to fill every inch of my being.

This was my family. This was my life.

And I would do anything to protect it.

twelve

CELESTINA

EMERGING FROM THE BEDROOM, Beckett held Emilia like she was the most precious thing in his universe, and a twisted ache of jealousy stabbed through me. How could I be envious of my own child? The guilt bit down hard. Sensing my turmoil, he shifted her to his other arm and wrapped his now free one around my waist, anchoring me to his side.

"I love you, Celestina," he said softly, his voice a balm to my frayed nerves. "Never doubt that."

A familiar voice broke the tender moment, cutting through the room like a knife. "Oh, goodie... looks like they made up." Antonio's snarky tone snapped my head in his direction. I felt a retort forming on my tongue, sharp and defensive, but then I noticed the crowded living room. Faces, some familiar and some not, watched us with various expressions—curiosity, relief, even suspicion.

Beckett's hold tightened, a silent question in his eyes as he whispered, "Whoa...you okay?"

I nodded, swallowing the lump in my throat. "Yeah, just surprised to see everyone." I glanced around the room, my gaze landing on a man I hadn't seen in far too long. My heart stuttered, and I slipped from Beckett's embrace, rushing across the room.

"Daddy."

His arms enveloped me, solid and safe, and I collapsed into them, the dam of my emotions breaking as tears spilled over. "Stellina," he murmured against my hair, his voice thick with emotion. "Little Star. I was so worried about you. Your mother and I...we were afraid you'd never find your way back to us, even with my precious *patata* in your arms."

I pulled back, wiping my cheeks. "Daddy, I want you to meet Beckett." I gestured toward him, feeling the tension simmer in the air between them.

My father's gaze was sharp, assessing. "I know who you are, Mr. Heart. But do they?" His eyes swept the room. "I didn't think so. My sons told me you'd returned, but is this just a game to you, or are you here to do right by my daughter? Because if you hurt her again, I will kill you myself."

Beckett's spine straightened. His jaw was set in determination. He responded in perfect Italian, his voice steady. *"Non sai niente su di me. Ma...L'unico motivo per cui sono qui è per lei. Preferirei strapparmi il cuore piuttosto che ferirla di nuovo. Hai la mia parola che lei è tutto ciò che mi interessa... beh, lei e mia figlia."* You know nothing about me. But...the only reason I'm here is because of her. I'd rather cut out my own heart than hurt her again. You have my word that she is all I care about—well, her and my daughter.

The room fell silent, shock rippling through those gathered. My father's stern expression softened, and he extended his hand. "Ahh…ne so più di te, ma questo è per un altro tempo e luogo. *Ottimo. Benvenuto in famiglia. Ora…diamo la caccia a questo mostro e troviamo l'altra mia figlia.*" *Ahh… I know more than you, but that is for another time and place. Very well. Welcome to the family. Now…let's hunt this monster and find my other daughter.*

Massimo gestured for us to sit. "Beckett, have a seat. Let's get you acquainted with everyone."

Handing Emilia back to me, Beckett pulled me down onto his lap, his protective arms wrapped around me like a shield. I scanned the room, taking in the mix of faces—some friendly, some not. Vincenzo, Antonio, Michael, Donny, Drew, Alex, Alec. A coalition of power, bound by blood and loyalty. But the real shock came when I noticed the men flanking my father—Lorenzo Bianchi and his father, Filippo Bianchi.

The air thickened with tension as introductions were made. Miguel Angel, head of the Sureños, his presence a testament to our expanding alliances. The Silva brothers from Chile, their sharp eyes missing nothing. And then, the Bianchis.

Beckett's body went rigid beneath me, and I glanced at him, worry twisting in my gut.

Lorenzo's voice was a sneer wrapped in disdain. "Mr. Heart," he began, his thick Italian accent dripping with contempt. "While we are here to help our longtime friends, we are not your friends. You tried to pit us against each other for a madman's gain."

"You're right." Beckett's voice was calm, steady. "But love won out. I would never do anything to hurt Celestina again."

His arms tightened around me, causing Emilia to whimper at the movement. "But your opinion of me doesn't matter. Hers does. I don't care if anyone here approves of me. It won't change the fact that she is mine, and I will do everything to protect her."

Filippo's hand rested on Lorenzo's shoulder, a quiet command for restraint. "He is right, Lorenzo. We are not here to make friends. We are here to destroy the man who threatens us all."

"Fine," Lorenzo spat. "But if you turn on us, I'll gut you like a pig."

"Hey, now," Vincenzo's voice cut through the tension. "If anyone is doing any gutting, it'll be me."

Antonio groaned, rubbing his temples. "Jesus, Vin."

"Enough," Massimo interjected, his tone brooking no argument. "Celestina, take Emilia downstairs. The girls are waiting for you."

I stiffened, the idea of being shut out sending a rush of anger through me. "Excuse me? This involves me as much as it does any of you."

Massimo's mouth opened, but Beckett spoke first, his voice gentle but firm. "Baby, please. Let us do this. Your safety—yours and Beck's—is what matters most right now. I promise to tell you everything later, but for now, let us protect you."

I took a deep breath, trying to quell the rising fear that gnawed at me. "Fine," I muttered, though the bitterness in my voice was palpable. "But if you keep anything from me, this," I motioned between us, "is over."

Pressing a kiss to his lips, I stood, my heart heavy. Beckett leaned forward, pressing another to Emilia's head.

"I love you both."

"Oh, God, just go," Vincenzo grumbled. "You're making me want to go home to my wife, and I can't leave this room."

Laughter bubbled up from somewhere deep inside me, easing a bit of the tension. I moved toward the stairs, glancing over my shoulder. "Suck it up, Vincenzo... or have you gone soft?"

The sound of something hitting the door as I closed it and the laughter erupting behind it made me smile The descent down the stairs felt heavier than it should, each step echoing my doubts and fears. When I reached the bottom, four sets of eyes turned toward me, concern etched in their faces.

"Got kicked out, did you?" Catarina's voice was soft, the understanding in her gaze almost undoing me.

I shrugged, the weight of everything pressing down on my shoulders. "I guess I needed to cool off," I whispered, my voice trembling as I slid Emilia into the bassinet. It felt like a lie; I was the one being left in the dark, shoved aside because I couldn't be trusted to hold it together.

Riley's arm wrapped around me, her touch warm and familiar. "We're all scared, Cee. But you're not alone."

I closed my eyes, willing the tears back, but the dam broke. The guilt, the fear, the self-loathing—all of it poured out, unstoppable and raw. "I'm the reason Carmela's gone, the reason Beckett had to come back, the reason Carlisle's dead. I don't deserve any of this."

The words were like a knife to my own heart, and I pulled away from Riley, grabbing the water bottle from the counter and hurling it at the wall. The kids screamed, their cries piercing the air like accusations, and I felt myself unraveling. I fell to the ground, the sobs tearing through me, uncontrollable, unstoppable.

"Cee," Catarina's voice was a plea, but I was beyond comfort, beyond reason. I crawled away from her, the despair swallowing me whole.

"I'm sorry, I'm so sorry." The words were a broken litany, a desperate apology to a world I felt unworthy of. I stumbled to my feet, fleeing to the bathroom, slamming the door behind me. The silence that followed was suffocating.

I didn't deserve this life. I didn't deserve any of it.

Opening the cabinet, I fumbled for the bottle of pills, my hands shaking so hard I almost dropped it. Michael's misery, my escape. Twisting off the cap, I poured the pills into my hand, staring down at them with a strange, detached calm.

Maybe the world would be better without me. Maybe Emilia would be better off without a mother who couldn't even keep her sister safe. I glanced at my reflection, the woman staring back a stranger. Broken. Unworthy.

Swallowing the pills dry, I turned on the faucet, letting the water wash the taste away. The knock on the door was distant, Catarina's voice muffled and desperate.

"Cee, please. Open the door."

But I was so tired. Tired of fighting, tired of pretending, tired of living.

I slid to the floor, letting the void take over as the darkness slowly closed in.

Maybe this was the only way to make things right.

Maybe this was the only way to find peace.

thirteen

BECKETT

LORENZO'S GAZE burned into me. His skepticism laced with disdain. "So, Beckett Heart," he began, his voice cutting through the room like a blade, "why should we believe anything you say? As soon as Manuel is dead, what's stopping you from leaving and betraying this family... betraying us?"

I glanced around the room, the eyes of powerful men fixed on me, each one weighing my worth. I swallowed the anger that clawed at my throat, forcing myself to keep my tone steady, controlled. "Sending Celestina away and staying away from her was like cutting out my own heart. I assumed I was shielding her, keeping her safe from Manuel, but it was a mistake—a mistake I will never make again. I won't leave her side, and I know her family is everything to her. My loyalty is to her first...and the family second."

Lorenzo's lips twisted into a cold smile. "And if it comes down to a choice between her life or yours? Would you lay down your life for her?"

I took a breath, locking eyes with him. "Have you ever been in love, Lorenzo?"

He shook his head, a shadow crossing his face. "No…I don't believe that is in the cards for me."

"Then you can't understand the depth of what I feel. Loving her is like breathing—it's not something I can control. I don't deserve her, not after the pain I caused, but I will spend every moment proving I'm worthy of her. I'd die for her without a second thought."

Lorenzo's jaw tightened, but it was Massimo who stepped in, his voice calm but firm. "He'll have his chance to prove his loyalty. Right now, we need to focus on finding Manuel and bringing Carmela home."

A flicker of pain crossed Lorenzo's face at the mention of Carmela. "We can't afford to lose time. We can't risk another funeral."

A man I hadn't noticed before, his hands clenched into tight fists, stepped forward, his voice strained. "How do we know she isn't already dead?"

"Alex," Massimo's voice was a warning, but the anguish in Alex's eyes was palpable. "We have to believe she's alive. We have to hold on to hope. Please."

The room grew still, the weight of Alex's question lingering in the air. I cleared my throat, drawing their attention. "I don't think she's dead. One of Manuel's men said something that didn't make sense."

Alex's eyes flashed with anger as he spat, "What did he say?"

"He said Manuel was planning to 'make an example' out of the other 'whore.' If you haven't received her body, then he hasn't killed her. He's likely sold her." The words felt like poison on my tongue, but they were necessary. "That's what he does."

Massimo's face paled. "Sold her?" He ran a hand through his hair, frustration etched into every line of his body. "I'm not sure that's any better."

"It's not, but it means she's alive. It buys us time."

"Antonio, call Alec. Get him to dig into the skin trade Manuel's running."

"We can help." A tall, honey-skinned man stepped forward, his presence commanding. "Cristian and Katya have been working to dismantle human trafficking rings. They have contacts who might know where Manuel's operating."

Massimo's gaze softened with a hint of gratitude. "Do whatever you need. Just find her."

"Matias," the man I now knew as Cristian turned to the one who'd spoken. "I'll get Katya up to speed."

"She's here?" Massimo's eyebrow lifted in surprise.

Matias shrugged with a smile. "All the wives are here. They wanted to be here for your women, just like yours were for them."

"Besides," a third man added, stepping beside Matias, "Everly and Ariel can help. Everly knows the logistics of how these bastards transport women, and Ariel's a genius with offshore accounts. She can help your tech guy trace the money."

"Damn," Vincenzo shook his head in disbelief. "Guess that leaves me and Miguel to shake down our Vegas contacts."

My eyes landed on the man standing in the shadows, his expression unreadable, exuding a quiet menace. He was a formidable presence, but I was no stranger to darkness myself. Our gazes locked, an unspoken challenge passing between us. He dipped his chin, and I returned the gesture, our silent understanding clear.

"Who the hell are you?" Filippo Bianchi's voice broke the tension as he eyed Miguel Angel warily. Miguel ignored him, but Giacomo Anastasi, Celestina's father, stepped forward, his voice steely.

"Filippo, Miguel is the head of the Sureños and has saved this family once before. He is a trusted ally. Disrespect him again, and I will let him show you what he is capable of."

Before Filippo could respond, the basement door slammed open, and Sofia Bianchi stumbled into the room, her face pale with fear.

"You…it's Celestina. Something's wrong."

Her words were a detonator to the bomb inside me. I was moving before I could process what I was doing, my feet barely touching the ground as I raced down the stairs. The scene that greeted me was chaos—Catarina was desperately trying to pry open the bathroom door with a knife.

"Beckett, thank God." Her voice was ragged with panic. "She's in there. She—she's not answering."

My heart plummeted. I banged on the door, shouting, "Celestina! Baby, can you hear me? Open the door!"

"She was upset," Catarina's voice cracked. "She was blaming herself for everything. I mentioned Alex, and it was like she shattered. She said she didn't deserve to live... and then she locked herself in there."

I didn't hesitate. Taking a step back, I kicked the door with every ounce of strength I had. It flew open, revealing a sight that would haunt me forever—Celestina, crumpled on the floor, an empty pill bottle beside her.

"Fuck," I breathed, dropping to my knees beside her. "How long?" My voice was a raw whisper.

"Thirty minutes, maybe," Catarina stammered, tears streaming down her face. "Get her out here, Beckett."

Scooping her limp body into my arms, I carried her to the living room, the world around me blurring into insignificance. Laying her on the floor, I pressed my fingers to her neck. Nothing.

"Celestina, baby, stay with me." I tilted her head back and blew air into her lungs, praying, begging for a response. I started chest compressions, my hands trembling as I pushed against her fragile body. Alex dropped beside me, his eyes red and desperate.

"Let me help," he choked out, and I nodded, switching off with him.

Massimo appeared, holding the pill bottle like it was a ticking time bomb. "Michael, how many were left?"

Michael's face twisted in anguish. "I don't know. Maybe six or seven. I never thought she'd—" His voice broke, and Antonio pulled him into a fierce embrace.

I focused on breathing life back into the woman who had become my everything. "Don't do this, Celestina. Don't leave me."

Catarina knelt beside me, a small bag in her hands. "Move," she ordered, her voice sharp. She slid a device up Celestina's nose and pressed the plunger. "Please, baby sis, come back to us."

"What did you give her?"

"Narcan," she replied, her voice shaking. "It can reverse the effects, but I don't know if it's too late."

I held Celestina's head steady, my heart thumping so forcefully it felt like it would explode. Seconds felt like hours. Then, with a gasp, her eyes flew open, and I fell back, my body sagging in relief as she struggled to breathe.

"I've got you, baby," I whispered, cradling her against my chest. "I've got you."

The room erupted into movement as the doctor arrived, a flurry of instructions and medical jargon I couldn't process. I couldn't let her go, couldn't loosen my grip on the woman who held my heart in her fragile hands.

"She's breathing. That's the first step," Dr. Luchasi murmured, his hands gentle but efficient. "We need to get her upstairs, hooked up to fluids. Can you carry her?"

"I'm not putting her down," I replied, my voice hoarse with emotion. "Tell me what to do."

With Celestina cradled in my arms, I stood, her weight so light it felt like she might disappear. I climbed the stairs, every step a promise I whispered to her soul. I wasn't going anywhere. Not now. Not ever.

As I laid her on our bed, I pressed a kiss to her knuckles, my heart breaking all over again. "Come back to me, baby. Emilia needs you. *I* need you."

Giacomo's voice, heavy with grief and determination, broke the silence. "Dr. Luchasi, will my daughter be okay?"

The doctor glanced at him. His eyes were shadowed with uncertainty. "She's breathing. That's the most important thing right now. I need to monitor her closely, but she's strong. We'll take it one minute at a time."

Nodding, Giacomo's gaze softened as he looked at me. "Take care of her, Beckett. I had my doubts about you, but I see now how much she means to you."

"She's everything," I whispered, holding her hand like a lifeline.

"Then do whatever it takes to bring her back," he said softly, his voice cracking. "Bring back my little star."

"I will," I vowed, pressing my lips to her hand, my heart in my throat. "I swear to you, I will."

The room emptied, the door closing softly behind them. Alone with her, I rested my forehead against the bed, the world narrowing to the sound of her breaths, the faint rise and fall of her chest.

"I'm sorry," I whispered, my voice breaking. "I'm so sorry, baby. But I'm here now. I'm not going anywhere. Please, Celestina, come back to me. We need you."

And for the first time in my life, I prayed—not for forgiveness or redemption—but for the chance to love her the way
she deserved. To show her that even the darkest hearts could
find their way back to the light.

fourteen

CELESTINA

A DENSE FOG enveloped the cavern, shrouding the space in an almost impenetrable gloom. The only sound was the faint murmur of voices echoing off the cold stone walls, a soft hum too low to decipher. I strained to focus, to pick apart the words or discern any familiar tone, but my mind felt sluggish, disconnected—as if I were submerged in water, every sound and thought distorted and blurred.

I flexed my fingers, willing them to find something solid, something real to anchor me. I stretched out my hand, grasping at the emptiness around me. Nothing but cold, damp air met my touch, slipping through my fingers like the shadows that danced at the edge of my vision. Panic prickled at the edges of my awareness. Why was I here? I couldn't remember how I'd ended up in this place, nor why my limbs felt heavy, almost immovable, as if bound by invisible chains.

My thoughts were a chaotic whirl, fragments of images and sounds flitting through my mind too quickly to grasp. Faces, voices—were they real, or just the remnants of a dream? Each attempt to recall something concrete was met with a suffocating blanket of confusion, stifling the rising panic, but also any hope of clarity.

I forced myself to take slow, measured breaths, trying to ground myself, to hold on to something real, but the exhaustion was overwhelming, seeping into my bones like a toxin. The urge to fight, to scream, to break free, dwindled with every passing second, until all that was left was a weary surrender.

The world around me seemed to blur further, the fog thickening, pressing in on me from all sides. My body felt heavy, my eyelids drooping despite the rising fear in my chest. I fought against the pull of oblivion, but it was like fighting against a powerful current, each surge pulling me deeper into the darkness.

And then, as if some unseen force decided my fate, I let go. The fight drained out of me, and I slipped back into the enveloping shadows, the murmur of voices fading into silence as the void swallowed me whole.

fifteen

BECKETT

THERE WERE many moments in my life where I'd felt fear, but nothing compared to the raw terror that gripped me when I found Celestina on the floor, unconscious and unresponsive. Her face had been drained of all color, and her body had seemed so frail, so lifeless. The image was seared into my mind like a brand, haunting me in every waking moment and tormenting me in the few hours I managed to sleep. More daunting than that sight, though, was having to press my lips to hers and breathe life into her. Each breath I forced into her lungs felt like a plea, a desperate bargain with the universe to give her back to me. Had I pushed her to this? Had my failure to protect her shattered her so completely that she'd felt the only escape was to end her life?

I tugged her hand to my lips, pressing a gentle kiss against her knuckles, willing her to feel my presence, to know I was here. The skin beneath my mouth was soft, too soft, a reminder of how fragile she was. Several times over the last few days, she'd come out of the unconscious state she'd been under, her eyes fluttering open for mere seconds, but they were empty, devoid of recognition or emotion. It was as if she was trapped somewhere far away, somewhere I couldn't reach. The fear of losing her—truly losing her—was suffocating.

Nestled in the crook of my arm, Emilia stirred, her tiny face scrunching as if she could sense the turmoil swirling around her. Two months ago, I couldn't have imagined this life— couldn't have believed that I'd be sitting here, holding my daughter, praying for the woman I loved to come back to me. I'd convinced myself that being away from Celestina was the best thing for everyone, that distance would protect her, but I had been so wrong. My absence had left her vulnerable, unguarded against the storm that had swept through her life.

"Beckett." Madison's voice cut through the heavy silence, and I glanced over my shoulder at her. Concern etched her features as she took in the sight of me, a man barely holding it together. "Take a break. I'll stay with her."

"I can't," I whispered, shaking my head as I turned back to Celestina. "I'm the reason she's here like this. It's been a week, Madison… a week, and she hasn't woken up. She hasn't looked at me, hasn't said a single word. What if she never does?"

"This isn't your fault," she said softly, sliding a chair across the floor and settling it beside me. "This is Manuel Costa's fault. He's the monster who did this, and when my husband and his brothers find him, he'll regret ever crossing our family."

"I'm so torn," I murmured, pressing my lips against my daughter's head, the weight of my decisions crushing me. "I want to hunt him down, make him pay for everything he's done. But I can't leave her. My father didn't care about my mother, and she died because of it. I don't want to be like him…I don't want to be the man who abandons the people he loves. I don't know how to be better than the blood running through me, but I know leaving her now would be wrong."

"You can leave her, and honestly, you should."

Her words snapped me out of my thoughts, anger flaring in my chest as I turned to glare at her. "What the fuck does that mean?"

Madison tilted her head, her eyes filled with a sympathetic pain that cut straight through me. "She did this because of the guilt she's been carrying, Beckett. She's never blamed you. She blames herself—blames herself for Carmela being taken, for Carlisle's death. She thinks she's the reason all of this happened, and it's destroying her."

Her voice cracked, and she looked away, her shoulders trembling. "Carlisle was my friend, Beckett. He was like a brother to me. He fought for her, died for her, and it kills me to know he's gone. I can't imagine the weight of that guilt on her shoulders. And while you're back, she doesn't know if it's for good. You told her you were staying, but that's going to take time to believe."

"I told her—"

"I know what you told her," she interrupted, her tone firm. "But you've got to understand—she's drowning in this guilt. She's been hurting since she woke up in the hospital. We all thought she was coping, but she was just hiding it. And that's on us, too. It's on her brothers for not seeing it, for not realizing she was trying to plan my wedding because she needed to stay busy, needed something to distract herself from the pain."

"Hidden?" I shifted Emilia in my hold, my heart clenching.

"She's been breaking right in front of us, and we missed it. We missed all the signs. We were so caught up in our own grief and anger, we didn't see what was happening to her. You and I both know what it's like to love someone and not be able to help them. This isn't just on you, Beckett. It's on all of us."

Her words struck a chord deep inside me, the truth of them resonating painfully. Over the past few days, Madison and I had discovered we were cousins, bound by blood and shared pain. Her father had been a loving parent until tragedy had turned him into a drunk, much like my own father. We'd both been lost, struggling in our own ways, and now we were connected by this fragile thread of family.

"There have been nights I've worried about Massimo," she continued, her voice a whisper of anguish. "He spaces out, and I can see the pain in his eyes. He's afraid, Beckett. Afraid of losing me, of losing our baby. I'm terrified that if we don't find Carmela, I'm going to lose him. He's building walls around himself, shutting me out. And when he shuts me out, my heart breaks. Because I can't lose him. I can't lose the man I love."

Her confession hit me like a blow to the stomach. I knew that kind of fear, that kind of desperation. It was the same fear that had driven me to push Celestina away, thinking I was protecting her when all I'd done was hurt her.

"So don't sit here," she pleaded, her hand reaching out to rest on my arm. "Let me do that. You go out there and find that bastard who's tearing this family apart. Because if you don't, he's going to destroy all of us."

"I'm sorry, Bella."

Massimo's deep voice startled us both, and Madison's head snapped up as he strode into the room.

"Massimo," she breathed, her voice trembling.

"Come here, Bella," he murmured, holding out his hand. She went to him without hesitation, and he wrapped her in his arms, pressing a kiss to her forehead. "I did not mean to make you feel afraid. You and our little one are everything to me. Yes, my family is important, but you will always come first." He kissed her softly, reverently, and I turned away, giving them the privacy they deserved. "Now, Beckett, my wife is right."

He crossed the room, scooping Emilia from my arms, making me tense. "Calm down. I need your help, so letting Madison take over here is necessary. She understands you, Beckett. And since you are family, trust us to have your back."

He handed my daughter to Madison, who held her gently, pressing a kiss to her tiny head.

"We have information and are planning a strike," he continued, his voice low and urgent. "We're going to bring him down, Beckett. We're going to end this."

I pressed my lips to Celestina's forehead, the coolness of her skin a painful reminder of how close I'd come to losing her. "I'm coming back for you, baby. Don't you give up on me."

Every step away from her felt like I was being torn in two, but I pushed down the pain and followed Massimo down the stairs. The living room was filled with grim faces, men ready for war. Vincenzo, Antonio, Michael, Donny, Alex, Filippo, and Lorenzo—each of them determined, each of them carrying the weight of loss and anger.

"You ready?" Vincenzo asked quietly, his eyes searching mine.

"Yes," I replied, my voice steady despite the turmoil inside me. "Where are we going?"

"To meet up with the Silva brothers. Cristian and Katya have found something. We're heading to Vin's place to get the details. Miguel will be there, too. He's got intel on Manuel."

We climbed into the cars. The hum of the engines was a stark contrast to the chaos in my mind. As we sped through the streets, I kept my thoughts on Celestina, on the promise I'd made to her. I would come back. I would bring her sister home. And I would make sure the man who'd caused all this pain never hurt anyone again.

I drew in a long breath, forcing myself to concentrate. This was for Celestina. For Carmela. For all the lives torn apart by one man's greed. As we stepped into the dining room, I saw the determination in everyone's eyes, felt the resolve in the air. This was a fight we were all ready for.

"So… What do you have?" I asked, my voice steady, my heart racing.

Katya's gaze met mine, her expression serious. "We have a location. An auction in Bogotá."

My heart hammered in my chest, the hope I'd been clinging to flaring to life. This was it. Our chance. I would find Carmela. I would bring her home.

And then I would destroy Manuel Costa.

But as my phone vibrated in my pocket, the world seemed to tilt. I pulled it out, my breath catching as I saw the name on the screen.

"She's awake," Catarina said, her voice trembling with relief.

The room seemed to spin as I stood, my heart pounding in my ears. "I'm on the way."

With one last look at the men gathered around, I turned and ran. I had a promise to keep.

sixteen

CELESTINA

MY MOUTH FELT DRY, as if I'd been chewing on a mouthful of cotton. My eyelids were so heavy, it was like they were weighed down with sandbags. I blinked slowly, the bright light piercing through my lashes and burning my eyes. I flinched, my head turning toward the noise beside me. Catarina sat in an uncomfortable-looking chair pushed up against the bed, her face etched with exhaustion, her eyes puffy and red.

"Catarina." My voice sounded like gravel, rough and broken, barely a whisper. I cleared my throat and tried again. "Cat."

Her eyes snapped open, and she was on her feet in an instant, moving toward me with a look of both relief and anger swirling in her gaze.

"Oh my God, Cee." Her voice trembled as she reached for me, her fingers gripping mine with a desperation that made my heart ache. "You're awake." But there was no mistaking the anger simmering beneath her relief. "Jesus Christ, Cee. You had us all terrified. Why didn't you tell us you were hurting this much? We would have helped you. You… you almost died." Tears welled in her eyes, and the sight of them tore at my soul. "I can't lose another sister, Cee. I can't."

I turned my head away, shame flooding through me. The weight of my guilt pressed down like a stone on my chest. "I'm sorry. I didn't think. I was just… I was just hurting too much. I've fucked everything up. I can't even do this right." The self-loathing in my voice was thick, wrapping around every word, choking me with its intensity.

"Oh, Cee." Catarina's arms came around me, pulling me into a hug that felt both too much and not enough. "You haven't messed anything up. You're hurting, and it's okay to be hurt. We'll find Carmela and bring her home. We'll get through this."

"Will we?" My voice broke, and I hated how weak I sounded, how lost.

Catarina pulled back, her expression hardening with determination. "Yes, we will." She took out her phone, her fingers trembling as she dialed. "I need to call Dr. Luchasi."

Kevin Luchasi had been the family doctor for as long as I could remember. He'd patched us up after countless scrapes and injuries, had been there when I'd recovered from my accident. And now, he'd be picking up my pieces once again. I rolled away from her, my eyes locking on the clear blue sky outside. It seemed mocking, the beauty of it, as if the world hadn't just fallen apart. I barely noticed the bed dip as he arrived.

"Celestina." His voice was calm and gentle, but it still sent a shiver of shame through me. He placed his hand on my shoulder, the warmth of his touch almost unbearable. "Let's look you over, okay?"

I nodded, rolling onto my back, my eyes squeezed shut against the overwhelming guilt and humiliation. "I know you don't want to, sweetheart, but I need you to open those beautiful brown eyes so I can assess you." His voice was a soothing balm, but it didn't stop the tears from welling up. "Do you know where you are?"

"Yes." My throat burned with the effort of speaking. "My house."

"That's right." His gaze was steady, patient. "Can you tell me what happened?"

Another tear slipped free, hot and unwanted. "I stole some of Michael's pain medication… and took it."

"And how much did you take, Celestina?"

"Maybe six or seven pills, I think." I shrugged weakly. "There weren't many in the bottle."

"Thank God for that." Catarina's voice was thick with emotion as she sat on the edge of the bed, her grip on my hand tightening. "I thought you were dead, Cee. I've seen a lot of shit in the ER, but seeing you like that…watching Beckett give you mouth-to-mouth… I thought I'd lost you."

The mention of his name made my heart clench painfully. "Beckett..." My voice trailed off, the reality of what I'd done overwhelming me like an avalanche. "He's going to leave me now, isn't he?"

Dr. Luchasi's expression softened with something like pity.

"You're lucky, Celestina. If Catarina hadn't administered Narcan, you wouldn't be here right now."

"What happens now?" I asked, my voice trembling.

"I'm recommending you see a therapist and that you not be left alone for the time being. You tried to take your own life, Celestina. That means you're still at risk. And I need to tell you that breastfeeding is no longer an option. Your body is still purging the drugs, and it could be dangerous for Emilia. We can't risk her safety."

His words were a knife to my heart. The thought of hurting my daughter made me feel like I was drowning in guilt. "Where is she? Where's Emilia?"

"She's fine, Cee. Madison has her downstairs. She's been taking care of her, so don't worry. We just need you to focus on getting better."

"And Beckett?" My voice was barely a whisper as I forced myself to ask the question. I needed to know, even if it shattered me.

"I called him. He's on his way back."

"He didn't leave?"

"No—" Catarina's answer was cut off by the sound of footsteps and then the voice I thought I might never hear again.

"I'm not leaving you, Celestina. I meant it when I said I'm here for the long haul."

The sound of his voice was like a lifeline, pulling me back from the edge of despair. I turned my head, my eyes filling with tears as I saw him standing in the doorway, his gaze locked on mine, fierce and unyielding.

"I love you, Cee," Catarina whispered, brushing a kiss across my forehead. "I'll bring Becks up to see you soon."

"I'll be back in a few hours to run some more tests," Dr. Luchasi said, his voice gentle. "But for now, you need to rest."

"Can I at least go to the bathroom? Maybe shower?" I asked, hating how weak I sounded.

"You'll need help, since I'm not removing the IV yet."

"I can help her," Beckett said, his voice steady and full of a conviction I didn't deserve. He sat on the edge of the bed, his hand finding mine and squeezing gently. "I'm not letting anything happen to her, Doc. I promise."

I turned my head away, the tears slipping free despite my best efforts. "I'm sorry," I whispered, my voice breaking.

"For what?"

"You shouldn't have to deal with me, Beckett. This is why you walked away, isn't it? So you wouldn't get caught up in my drama, my mess."

"Look at me, Celestina." His hand moved down my arm, his touch warm and grounding. "Please, roll over."

Slowly, I turned to face him, my heart aching with the weight of everything I wanted to say but couldn't. He shifted closer, his hand cupping my cheek, his eyes boring into mine with an intensity that stole my breath.

"I walked away because I thought I was protecting you. I thought I was keeping you safe. And that choice nearly got you killed, got your sister taken. I can't take back what I did, but I can make damn sure you're not alone anymore. This isn't your fault. It's not even my fault. It's Manuel Costa's doing. But promise me something, Celestina."

"What?" I asked, my voice small and broken.

"I need you to promise me you'll tell me if it ever gets this bad again. Emilia can't lose you. I can't lose you." He leaned down, pressing his lips to mine in a kiss so tender it brought fresh tears to my eyes. "Please."

"I'll try," I whispered against his mouth, the words a fragile promise.

"Let's get you cleaned up, baby." His voice was a soothing balm, and as he helped me sit up, the room spun slightly. "I'll do anything for you."

He scooped me into his arms, and I clung to him, my body trembling with exhaustion and fear. Beckett carried me into the bathroom, gently setting me down on the counter. I watched him as he moved, his every action careful, deliberate. He turned on the shower, testing the water before turning back to me.

"Did you think I'd let you get in alone?" he asked, raising an eyebrow as he stripped down to his boxers. The sight of him, so strong and steady, made something in my chest loosen.

"Okay," I whispered, feeling strangely vulnerable.

He lifted me into his arms again, carrying me into the shower and setting me down on the built-in bench. His hands were gentle as he washed me, the soap and water washing away the grime of the past few days. He was thorough but tender, his touch never lingering too long in any one place. When he moved to wash my hair, the sensation of his fingers massaging my scalp made me sigh, the tension seeping out of my body.

"Sorry," I mumbled, embarrassed by the sound that had escaped my lips.

"Don't be," he said softly. "Close your eyes."

The water cascaded over me, warm and soothing, and for the first time in what felt like forever, I felt clean. When he was done, he turned off the water and wrapped me in a towel, drying me off with a gentleness that made my heart ache.

"I'm going to take care of you, Celestina," he murmured, his voice a promise. "You and Emilia. Always."

And after not believing for so long, I finally trusted him.

seventeen

BECKETT

THE SHARP INTAKE of breath against my chest told me she hadn't been prepared for what I was saying. I could almost feel the shock reverberating through her body. Celestina had believed Carmela was dead, and the possibility that she might still be alive was both a relief and a torment. I ran my fingers through her hair, taking a steadying breath before continuing, knowing I was about to lay bare a painful truth.

"Manuel Costa is deeply entrenched in the skin trade. Cristian Silva and Matias's wife, Katya, have spent the last year fighting to dismantle these trafficking rings in South America. When they found out about you and that Manuel was involved, they didn't hesitate to come and help. To be honest, I didn't expect them to find much. Manuel is more insidious than his brother Jose ever was. I've been chasing him for a year with nothing to show for it. Now I understand why… his operations are mainly out of Colombia."

"Colombia?" Her voice trembled, a mix of disbelief and hope. "You think my sister is there?"

"Yes. And thanks to Cristian, we're getting an invitation to an upcoming event in Bogotá. Miguel will be going with us, along with several of his men. We're going to bring her back."

"What about the others?" Her voice cracked, and I could hear the fear threading through her words. "What about all the other women?"

"For now, the only goal is to get Carmela out of there. If we can take down the whole operation, we will, but Carmela is our priority."

"You keep saying 'we'... does that mean you're going?" The fear in her eyes was palpable, a mirror of the fear that had gripped my heart ever since I found her on the floor.

"I have to go, Cee. I need to finish this. Manuel threatened something I love and took another, thinking it was you."

Her body shuddered against mine, the weight of everything finally breaking through the dam of her resolve. Her tears soaked into my skin, each one like a dagger slicing through my heart. A soft knock on the door drew my attention away from her for a moment.

"Come in."

I adjusted her in my arms, fully aware of how fragile she looked, how broken. I was shirtless, holding her in a bed she'd nearly died in. It was a raw moment, but I didn't care. I needed this connection, needed her to feel it, too. Catarina and Madison stepped into the room, followed by the rest of her family. Shifting so I could sit up against the headboard, I helped her sit with me, bracing her as she turned to face them.

This was going to be difficult, but she needed to see that she wasn't alone in this.

"I thought seeing your daughter would help." Madison stepped forward, holding Emilia in her arms. "She's been fed and changed, but she needs her mommy."

The room felt electric with tension as I took Emilia from Madison and pressed a soft kiss to her head. Her tiny, warm body felt like hope in my arms as I turned to Celestina.

"Here, baby. Hold our daughter."

Celestina's sob tore through the room, raw and filled with pain, as she reached out, her arms trembling. Everyone watched, but I couldn't look away from her face as a torrent of emotions flashed across her features—guilt, fear, love. Her gaze was locked on Emilia, the love shining in her eyes almost painful to witness.

"I'm so sorry, baby girl," she murmured, her voice trembling as she looked up at me, her eyes haunted. "How could I even think of leaving her? I'm a horrible mom."

"No, you're not." Massimo's voice cut through the room, firm and steady. "You're struggling, Cee, and we should have seen it."

"Non osare dirlo, Celestina. Sei la cosa più preziosa di questo mondo. Tu e i tuoi fratelli e sorelle siete la cosa più preziosa che ho. Ti amo piccola ragazza." *Don't you dare say it, Celestina. You are the most precious thing in this world. You and your brothers and sisters are the most precious thing I have. I love you, little girl.* His voice was a gentle command, his words a fierce declaration of love and protection.

Celestina's head whipped toward the door, her father's presence looming large, his eyes filled with the kind of anguish only a parent could feel.

"Padre. Mi vergogno tanto di me stesso." *Father. I am so ashamed of myself.*

"No. I won't hear it, Celestina." He switched to English. His tone was unyielding. "There is nothing to be ashamed of in feeling pain. And if anyone in this room makes you feel that way, I'll have them thrown out—family or not."

"He's right, Cee." Vincenzo stepped forward, kneeling beside the bed. "You're our baby sister. We should have seen this. Maybe we should have dragged him back here sooner. We'll never know. What we do know is we need to focus on finding Carmela and helping you get better." He leaned in, pressing a kiss to her forehead before turning his sharp gaze on me. "And as for you, Beckett, I will gut you if you hurt her again."

"Vin, no." Celestina's voice was a fragile plea, her hand reaching out to him.

"He's got the right," I said softly, holding her tighter. "But I swear to all of you, I won't hurt her again. I love her with everything I am. Without her…without both of them, there is no me. I'll set the world on fire to keep them safe."

Vincenzo's eyes softened, just slightly, and he nodded. "Good. In the morning, we leave."

One by one, they came forward to offer their love and support, each word a balm to the raw wounds on her heart. When they finally left us alone, the room felt strangely empty. She didn't say much, even when I took our daughter from her arms and laid her in the crib. Her silence spoke louder than words, and it scared me, the way she seemed to retreat inside herself, her gaze distant.

"What's going on in that head of yours?"

She let out a shuddering breath, her eyes closing as if it took all her strength to speak. "You're leaving me, aren't you?"

"Oh, baby." I slid back into bed beside her, pulling her into my arms as gently as I could. "I have to go. I need to see this through, but I promise you, I'm coming back."

"You promise?" Her voice wavered, a tear slipping free and soaking into the sheets.

"I promise. And when I come back, I'm going to marry you."

"Marry me?" Her eyes flew open, wide and full of disbelief.

"Yes. I've wasted too much time. I want you to be my wife, Celestina."

"I'd like that, Beckett." She shifted closer, pressing her cheek against my chest, her voice a fragile whisper. "What will you do when you give up everything for me?"

"Don't you get it, Celestina? You are everything. You and Emilia are my world. Once I know you're both safe, we can start our life together."

A soft knock interrupted us, and Dr. Luchasi stepped into the room, his presence a calm reassurance.

"Sorry to intrude, but I wanted to let you know that your blood work looks good, Celestina. I'll be removing your IV now." He moved quickly, his hands sure and steady as he worked. "You're lucky, you know. A little longer, and we might not be having this conversation."

"Thank you," she whispered, her voice small and raw.

"Just focus on getting better," he said, his smile gentle as he glanced at the crib. "You have a beautiful daughter."

As he left, I turned back to Celestina, brushing my thumb over her cheek. "I love you, Cee."

"I love you, too." Her voice was soft, but the smile she gave me was the first real one I'd seen in days. "Beckett?"

"Yeah, baby?"

"Will you kiss me?"

Her timid request stole the breath from my lungs. "You never have to ask, Celestina."

I leaned down, capturing her lips in a kiss that was full of every promise I could make, every vow I wanted to keep. This kiss was more than just a kiss. It was the beginning of our future. One I would fight like hell to make sure we had.

Because there was no future without her in it. Not for me. Not ever.

CELESTINA

WAKING up in Beckett's arms was a bittersweet reminder of what I'd almost thrown away—of the love and life I would've left behind if I'd succeeded in taking my own life. The guilt of that realization felt like a weight on my chest, constricting and unrelenting. But I couldn't afford to dwell on that right now. My daughter needed me, and so did Beckett. With a resolve I hadn't felt in days, I slid out of bed, trying not to wake him as I padded over to Emilia's crib.

She was making those sweet baby noises, the kind that hinted she was just moments away from a full-on cry, and I wanted to get to her before that happened. I bent down, lifting her gently into my arms, her tiny body warm and comforting against mine. Despite everything, she was my anchor.

"How is she?" Beckett's voice, husky and rugged, washed over me. He was sitting up now, the sheets pooling around his waist, giving me a perfect view of his scarred but beautiful chest. He looked like he'd just walked out of a dream, every inch of him radiating strength and warmth.

"Happy," I murmured, smiling down at Emilia as she grasped my finger in her little hand.

"Good. And you?" He watched me with that intense gaze, the one that always made me feel like I was the only person in the world.

"Better… feeling guilty, but I'm glad to be holding her in my arms and having you here with me."

He crossed the floor in a few strides, wrapping his arms around both me and Emilia, pulling us into his solid embrace. He pressed a tender kiss to our daughter's head, then tilted my chin up and captured my lips with his. It was a gentle kiss, filled with reassurance and love, the kind that spoke more than words ever could.

"There's no place I'd rather be," he whispered against my lips. "We should get dressed and head downstairs. There's a lot to get ready before I leave."

The words hurt, and I had to fight to keep my emotions in check. "Before you leave…" My voice cracked, betraying me. "Sorry… I know you have to do this."

"Hey," he said softly, his finger lifting my chin so I had no choice but to meet his gaze. "I'm coming back to you, Cee."

I nodded, unable to trust my voice. My throat felt tight, and I knew if I spoke, I'd burst into tears. Instead, I shuffled past him, carrying Emilia over to the bed and laying her down gently.

"Can you grab me a diaper?" I asked, my voice still shaky.

Beckett let out a deep breath, but he didn't say anything. I knew he was struggling, unsure of how to handle my fragility, but I didn't want him to tiptoe around me. I needed him to be strong, especially now, when he was about to go into something dangerous.

"Here," he said, handing me the diaper. His eyes bore into mine, intense and unwavering. "Don't hide from me, Cee. If you want to scream, scream. If you want to cry, then cry. Don't shut me out again, okay?"

"Okay," I whispered, focusing on changing our daughter. "I'm scared."

"I know you are, and I'd be lying if I said I wasn't, too. But you're going to have the best protection with you while I'm gone. Your brothers will make sure nothing happens to you."

I looked up at him, confusion mingling with my fear. "Wait… they're not going?"

"No." He shook his head, his expression grave. "They're staying with you. This is a family matter, and you and Emilia are their priority."

We quickly got ready and headed downstairs. The atmosphere in the house was charged, a palpable tension hanging in the air. Walking into a room full of powerful men, all eyes on us, was daunting. I felt Beckett's arm tighten around my waist as he led me to the head of the table, where he took a seat and pulled me onto his lap. Emilia squirmed in my arms, her presence a reminder of what was at stake.

"Celestina," my father said, standing from his seat and coming to kneel facing me. He took my hands in his, his eyes shining with a mixture of love and pain. "Please don't carry this guilt, my sweet girl. None of this is your fault. And with the help of these men, we will get your sister back and destroy the man who dared to come after our family."

His words seemed to have a calming effect on me, but I couldn't completely let go of the guilt that clung to me. "I'm sorry for being a coward, Padre, but no more. I am an Anastasi, and I will not cower to Manuel or his men again."

He took Emilia from my arms, his expression softening as he cradled her against his chest. "We will ensure your safety and hers. No one will ever threaten our family again."

"Especially since we are forging a new era." Filippo Bianchi stood, his voice resonating with authority. "Lorenzo will take control of Reno, giving your family another ally here in the U.S. Between the Bianchis and the strength of Miguel Angel, we will form a stronghold unlike anything we've had before."

This was monumental. Filippo was sending his only son to the States to establish a new faction of the Italian mafia. I glanced at Miguel, noticing the way his eyes lingered on Sofia. She looked at him with the same intensity, and I prayed that whatever was brewing between them wouldn't lead to conflict. The last thing we needed was more bloodshed.

The conversation turned to logistics, strategies on how to infiltrate the auction. I tried to follow along, but the plan they were outlining sounded dangerous—too dangerous.

"Wait," I interrupted, my heart pounding. "Did you say you're bringing a woman as a cover?"

"Yes," Miguel replied. "Many of these men bring women to show their dominance. Gael, my second-in-command, along with Alex and Beckett, will be attending. Gael will pose as a buyer with his 'slave,' while Alex and Beckett will be his guests."

My heart dropped at the thought. "What woman would volunteer for that?"

"Me." Sofia's voice was calm, but her eyes blazed with determination. "I'm the only one with the training and willingness to cut off a man's balls if he tries to touch me."

"No," I gasped, horror lacing my voice. "Sofia, you can't do that. It's too dangerous."

"She is right, Princessa," Miguel stepped closer to Sofia, his tone intense. "I would never have agreed to this if I'd known. You can't put yourself in that kind of risk."

In a flash, Sofia had him on his back, straddling him with a blade pressed against his throat. "If you wanted me on my back, Princessa, all you had to do was ask," Miguel murmured, his eyes dark with a mix of admiration and something deeper.

"Do not underestimate me, *maiale*. I will cut your throat before you even know what's happening."

I couldn't help but snort at the scene. It was absurdly surreal, but somehow, it lightened the tension just a little.

"Sorry," I said, covering my mouth with my hand. "It's just… I wasn't expecting that."

"Don't worry, Celestina." Sofia stood, smoothing her dress as if nothing had happened. "I'll make sure your sister is avenged, one way or another."

As she walked out, Miguel's eyes followed her, filled with

something I hadn't seen in a long time—hope. The clearing of a throat brought his attention back to the room.

"What?" he snapped, glaring at Lorenzo, who had a murderous expression on his face.

"Stop staring at my sister's ass. She is off-limits to you."

Miguel's smirk was dangerous. "I think that's her decision, chico."

"Enough," I interjected, exhaustion pulling at my voice. "We need to focus on getting Carmela back."

"You're right, Celestina." Lorenzo's anger dissipated, replaced by a look of remorse. "I'm sorry."

"I need to go feed Emilia. Beckett, come find me when you're done here. Please don't leave without saying goodbye."

"I would never leave without saying goodbye," he stated, his voice fierce with promise. "Are you sure you're okay going down to the basement?"

"Yes." I forced a smile, wanting to ease his worry. "I need to face it, Beckett. I'll talk to someone if it gets too hard. I love you."

"I love you, too. Just take it easy, okay?" His eyes were soft as he looked at me, and for a moment, I let myself believe that everything would be okay.

Leaving the room, I took slow, measured steps down the stairs, clutching Emilia close. My heart hammered in my chest as I approached the basement—the place where I'd nearly lost everything. When I stepped inside, Catarina was the first to see me. She rushed over, pulling me into a tight hug.

"I'm so glad you're okay, Cee."

I pulled back, shaking my head. "I'm sorry, Catarina. I'm so sorry you had to go through that. I didn't think…I wasn't thinking."

"Don't apologize, Cee. Do you know how many times I've had to patch up our brothers? It's part of the job description in this family. I'm just glad I could help."

We spent the next few hours talking and laughing, the light-heartedness a welcome distraction. When Donny came down and found Catarina covered in baby poop, his horrified expression had us all in stitches. For a little while, it felt normal—like we weren't all living under the shadow of a man who wanted to destroy us.

But even as we laughed, a part of me couldn't shake the fear that this peace was only temporary. That, despite Beckett's promises, I would be left alone again.

Later, when Beckett came to find me, his arms wrapped around my waist as I stood with Emilia in my arms, his warmth and strength grounded me.

"This will be us soon, Celestina. I promise you that. I've already talked with your brothers, and I'm going to be working with the family when I get back."

"Doing what?" I asked, turning to face him, my heart clenching with a mixture of fear and hope.

"Whatever the family needs." He pressed a kiss to my lips, his eyes filled with a determination that made me believe, even if just for a moment, that everything would be okay. "How are you feeling?"

"Tired, but good. It's hard to believe I'm standing here, a week after…" My voice trailed off, the memory of my suicide attempt still raw and painful. I'd almost lost everything; almost left the people I loved behind. The guilt and shame still gnawed at me, but I knew I had to push through it.

"Whatever you're thinking, stop." Beckett kissed my forehead, his voice gentle but firm. "We don't blame you for what happened, Cee. You need to let it go, too. Talk to the therapist, please. We need you here… Emilia and I need you."

"I will," I promised, wrapping my arms around his waist, holding him as if he might disappear. "Let's go to bed. It's late."

As we climbed the stairs to our room, leaving Emilia in the capable hands of Massimo and Madison, I felt a flicker of hope—a fragile, tentative thing that I was afraid to fully embrace.

Once inside, Beckett turned on the stereo, filling the room with a soft, soothing melody. He moved toward the bed, but I stopped him, reaching out to take his hand.

"Beckett." His name came out as a whisper, a plea.

"Celestina?" His brows furrowed in concern as he cupped my cheek. "What is it, baby?"

"You," I breathed, closing my eyes and leaning into his touch. "I just need you."

His lips found mine, and the world melted away. In that kiss, I felt the promise of tomorrow, the strength to face whatever lay ahead. Beckett was my rock, my sanctuary. And as I held him close, I knew that no matter what happened, we would face it together. Because without him, without Emilia, I was nothing.

And I wasn't willing to let go of that ever again.

nineteen

BECKETT

WITHOUT THINKING, I closed the distance between us, my lips meeting hers in a kiss that felt like it had the power to heal. As we moved together, the sound of Rihanna's "Stay" filled the room, the lyrics echoing the intensity of what we were about to do. We were both broken, both wounded, but somehow, we had found something pure in each other, a light in the darkness that we'd been stumbling through for so long. Every touch, every brush of skin against skin, made my breath catch and my heart pound in my chest.

"Are you sure?" I asked, my voice a rough whisper as I traced my fingers down her arm, feeling her shiver beneath my touch.

"Yes," she breathed, her voice steady despite the tremor in her hands.

She reached for the hem of my shirt, pushing it up my torso, her hands a little hesitant but determined. I lifted my arms, helping her strip it off, and when her fingers moved to my belt, fumbling as she tried to unbuckle it, my heart clenched at the sight of her vulnerability. She was giving herself to me completely, trusting me with her body and soul.

When she finally managed to undo my pants, her hand slid beneath the waistband, her fingers wrapping around me. A sharp hiss escaped my lips as she touched me, my cock twitching in her grasp. It took every ounce of control to step back and strip off the rest of my clothes, the need to feel her skin against mine nearly overwhelming.

"Take off your clothes...all of them," I murmured, my voice laced with raw desire.

Her eyes never left mine as she slipped off her leggings, then unhooked her bra, the soft fabric sliding down her arms and revealing the perfection of her body. Every inch of her called to me, and I couldn't help but reach out, wanting to touch, to feel, to claim her as mine. But before I could, she dropped to her knees, her hands covering mine as she guided my strokes, her tongue darting out to lick along the length of my shaft. The sensation sent a jolt of pleasure through my body, my legs shaking with the effort to stay standing.

"Fuck," I groaned, my hips bucking forward as she took me into her mouth, her warm, wet heat enveloping me. The sight of her, head bobbing as she sucked me down to the base, was almost too much to handle.

"Stop," I rasped, gripping her shoulders and pulling her to her feet. "I want to be inside you when I come, baby."

I lifted her and tossed her onto the bed, my mouth finding her center the moment her back hit the mattress. The taste of her was intoxicating, her sweet essence coating my tongue as I licked and sucked, my fingers plunging deep into her. Her cries echoed in the room, her body arching off the bed as I pushed her closer and closer to the edge.

"Let it go, baby," I urged, my voice a low growl against her slick folds. "I want to feel you fall apart around me."

She shattered, her body convulsing as her orgasm tore through her, her scream filling the space between us. I didn't waste a second, climbing over her and plunging deep inside her, the tight heat of her pussy squeezing me like a vice. Our bodies moved in a rhythm that felt ancient, primal, like we were made for this, for each other.

"Fuck," I grunted, my pace relentless as I drove into her again and again. The sound of our skin slapping together, the heady scent of sex filling the air—it was almost too much, but I held on, waiting for her, needing her to come with me.

"Let go, butterfly," I whispered against her ear, nipping at the delicate skin of her neck. "Let me feel you explode around my cock."

She obeyed, her body tightening around me as she came with a force that left us both breathless. Her cries of pleasure, the feel of her nails digging into my back, sent me over the edge, my own release tearing through me like a storm. I came deep inside her, the world falling away until there was nothing left but the two of us, lost in the bliss of each other.

Collapsing beside her, I pulled her into my arms, the after-math of what we'd just shared leaving us both trembling. I pressed soft kisses to her shoulder, my heart swelling with an emotion I hadn't dared to name until now.

"I'm going to marry you, Celestina—soon."

"What?" She half-turned, her eyes wide with surprise and still glazed with the pleasure we'd just shared. "Are you serious?"

"More than anything in my life," I said, my voice steady, my heart pounding with certainty. "I want you to be mine forever, butterfly."

Her smile was like the sun breaking through the clouds, and when her eyes filled with tears, I felt my own chest tighten with emotion. "Okay," she whispered, her voice trembling with happiness.

Rolling over, she climbed on top of me, her lips finding mine in a kiss that felt like a promise. As she slid down onto me, her body taking me in inch by inch, I knew I'd never be the same. She moved above me, her rhythm desperate, her hands braced on my chest as she chased her release.

I reached between us, my thumb finding her clit, and as soon as I touched her, she cried out, her body shaking with the force of her orgasm. I followed her over the edge, my release exploding inside her, a hot rush that felt like it would never end.

When it was over, she collapsed against my chest, her breathing ragged, her body still trembling. I wrapped my arms around her, holding her close, my heart so full it felt like it might burst.

"That was…" She trailed off, her voice full of awe.

"Out of this world," I finished for her, pressing a kiss to her temple. "I love you, butterfly."

"Butterfly?" She laughed softly, the sound like music to my ears.

"Yes, butterfly. You've emerged from your cocoon into this amazing woman, Celestina. You're like a monarch, gracing the world with your beauty—and you're all mine. I don't know what I did to deserve you, but I'm damn sure glad I have you."

Her eyes softened, her fingers tracing the lines of my face. "Will you tell me about your life?"

"It's not pretty." I blew out a breath, my fingers trailing down her shoulder. "My dad was a drunk who beat my mom to death, leaving me an orphan. His family cut him off long before I was born. He died in prison not too long after I joined the Marines, hoping to be better than him… only I wound up in prison myself, after making a bad decision that got men on my team killed. I was held responsible for disobeying an order and dishonorably discharged after serving a five-year sentence. When I got out, I had nothing. No family, no money…"

Her eyes were wide, her expression filled with sympathy and love. "What happened then?"

"One night, I met a man who was looking for someone with particular skills—skills I possess."

"A hitman."

"Yes." I nodded, my heart heavy with the memories. "I'm not proud of my choices, Butterfly, but they led me to you, so I won't apologize for the man I was."

"You've met my family. I have no room to talk, Beckett." She leaned up, pressing a soft kiss to my lips. "My grandfather was the don of an Italian mafia crime syndicate. My father took over for him, and now Massimo runs things here. We've seen our share of destruction."

"Yeah, but you were born into it. I chose it. There's a big difference. Hell, I kidnapped you because I was hired to. I knew it was wrong, but I couldn't help myself. The moment you ran from my car and rolled down that hill, I knew my life was going to change."

"I love you, Beckett. Nothing will change that. Not your past, not your future. As long as you love me back, I'll stand by your side until death."

I held her tighter, feeling the truth of her words sink into my soul. "I'll always love you, Celestina. And I'll prove it to you every day for the rest of our lives."

As her breathing evened out, I made a silent vow to bring Carmela home. After everything I'd done, I owed it to her and her family. And if it was the last thing I did, I would make sure Manuel Costa paid for every drop of pain he'd caused the woman I loved.

BECKETT

LEAVING Celestina behind felt like leaving my heart on the tarmac. Every step away from her was a battle against the primal urge to turn back, to stay and hold her and never let go. But the necessity of what I was about to do loomed larger than my own needs. It wasn't just about me or even her anymore. It was about righting the wrong that had shattered her world and ripped her sister away. It was about finding Carmela and bringing her home.

The hum of the engines reverberated through the cabin of Matias Silva's private jet as we soared above the Gulf of Mexico, heading toward Bogotá. The atmosphere inside was tense, charged with a shared, unspoken determination. Everyone on board knew what was at stake. To my left, Alex stared out the window, his jaw clenched, hands fisted in his lap. Across from us, Cristian and Katya Silva huddled together, whispering in urgent tones over a stack of documents and maps. They were methodical, almost clinical, as they prepared us for what was to come.

Sofia and Lorenzo Bianchi sat a few rows back, their expressions grim, while Miguel Angel and his second-in-command, Gael Alcaraz, ran through the tactical layout of the warehouse. It was clear that Gael was on edge, his eyes flicking over to Sofia every few minutes, as if he were preparing for a battle that had nothing to do with the mission at hand. Sofia would be acting as Gael's slave at the auction, a dangerous role that none of us took lightly. It was a ruse, a sick and twisted game where real lives were at stake, and I couldn't shake the gnawing worry that something would go horribly wrong.

I forced myself to focus on my own role. I'd be positioned outside the warehouse, hidden in the shadows with my rifle, ready to take out any threats. The risk of being recognized was too high for me to go inside, especially with Manuel Costa still gunning for my head. It was a necessary precaution, but one that left a bitter taste in my mouth. The thought of Carmela being auctioned off like a piece of meat while I waited outside made me want to tear the whole place apart with my bare hands.

As soon as we touched down, the adrenaline kicked in. There was no time to dwell on emotions or doubts. We were on a strict timetable, and every second counted. Matias had arranged for a team of his men to transport the weapons and gear we'd need. They were professionals, men who knew what they were doing, and their presence was a lifeline. Still, the knowledge that they were there because they'd been dealing with monsters like Manuel for years only heightened my anxiety.

Inside the hotel suite, Cristian and Katya laid out a dossier on each of the women who would be auctioned. I felt a cold shiver slide down my spine as I read through the details—names, ages, photos. Fifteen women, each with a story of stolen freedom and shattered dreams, reduced to mere commodities to be sold to the highest bidder. And there, among them, was Carmela's photo, a haunting reminder of why we were here.

"She's been gone for nearly three months," Cristian said softly, his voice laced with a sadness that mirrored my own. "We don't know what condition she'll be in when we find her."

The unspoken words hung heavy in the air. *If* we find her. Because despite all our planning, despite every piece of intel and every strategic maneuver, there were no guarantees. The thought of what she might have endured—rape, beatings, drugs to keep her compliant—made my blood boil. It took every ounce of control not to let the rage consume me. This wasn't just about revenge anymore. It was about bringing a sister, a daughter, a person, back to the people who loved her.

"All right, you four need to get ready," Cristian instructed, his tone brisk as he laid an ornate, gold-embossed invitation on the bed. "This is your ticket inside. The event starts at ten."

"Great," Miguel muttered, his eyes dark with fury as he glanced at the items. "They act like this is some sort of fucking gala."

His words were a bitter echo of what we were all thinking. The sheer mockery of dressing up to bid on human lives was enough to make anyone sick. But we had to play the part if we wanted to get inside and save her.

"Are your men in position?" Miguel asked, turning to Cristian.

"Yes. They arrived last night and have set up a perimeter around the warehouse. Beckett, Marco will meet us there to show you the best place to set up."

"Fine."

I busied myself with adjusting my gear, pulling on the bullet-proof vest over my black shirt. It felt heavy, a physical reminder of the weight of what we were about to do. The sound of the bathroom door slamming open snapped my attention up, and I froze at the sight before me.

Sofia stepped out, dressed—or rather, barely dressed—in a skimpy black leather outfit that was more straps than fabric. The sight of her, bold and defiant in six-inch stilettos, was enough to turn heads. Even I, who was hopelessly in love with Celestina, couldn't deny how striking she looked. But the expression on Miguel's face was pure fury.

"No," he growled, his voice low and dangerous. "You are not going like that, princessa."

Sofia sauntered over, her hips swaying with every step, and stopped in front of him. "You don't get a say," she shot back, her voice cool and unyielding.

In an instant, Miguel had her by the wrist, pulling her into the bathroom and slamming the door shut behind them. Lorenzo moved as if to intervene, but Gael stepped in front of him, raising a hand.

"Don't," he said firmly. "He won't hurt her, but they need to work this out."

"Work what out?" Lorenzo snapped. His frustration was palpable.

"Oh, come on, gringo. Don't be stupid. Anyone with eyes can see the sexual tension between them. He's losing his shit because she's putting herself in danger, and she's not handling his overprotectiveness well."

The door flew open, and Sofia stormed out, her hair mussed, lips swollen, a telltale flush staining her cheeks. It didn't take a genius to figure out what had happened behind that door. Miguel followed a moment later, his jaw clenched tight, a dangerous glint in his eyes.

"We good?" I asked, my voice steady as I looked between them.

"Yes," Sofia bit out, her chin lifting defiantly. "Let's get this over with."

She turned on her heel, stalking toward the door, and Miguel's gaze followed her, dark and possessive. "And if you ever pull that stunt again," Sofia called over her shoulder, "I'll bite your tongue off."

Miguel shrugged, his lips curving into a dangerous smile. "Sounds kinky." He glanced at Gael. "Keep her safe. We have unfinished business."

"Yes, sir."

Lorenzo muttered something in Italian, throwing his hands up in frustration. Katya just smirked, the scene unfolding in front of us clearly more entertaining than she'd expected. "I forgot how much fun this shit was," she said, chuckling as she followed Sofia out.

Alex was already by the door, his face tight with barely contained fear and determination. "You sure you're okay doing this?" I asked, placing a hand on his shoulder.

"I have to be," he replied, his voice hoarse. "I didn't even get the chance to tell her I loved her, Beckett. Do you know how that feels—to love someone and not know if they'll ever know it?"

"Yeah," I said softly, the memory of Celestina's fragile body in my arms as I fought to bring her back from the brink flooding my mind. "I know exactly how that feels."

"You need to be prepared," I warned, my voice rough. "She won't be the same. This changes people."

"I don't care," he said fiercely, his eyes burning with a fire that almost broke my heart. "I'll walk through fire to bring her back, and I'll stand by her as she heals."

"And if she still walks away?"

"At least I'll know I did everything I could to make her feel whole. If she doesn't want me after that, I'll love her from a distance."

I squeezed his shoulder, feeling the strength and desperation in his words. "Then let's bring her home."

The drive to the warehouse was silent, each of us lost in our own thoughts. The last time I'd been in Colombia, I'd been wearing a Marine uniform, fighting a different war. But the ghosts of that time had nothing on what we were facing now. This was a war of a different kind, fought not with guns and bombs, but with human lives.

As Cristian pulled the car onto a gravel road, my pulse quickened. He stopped the car, and I climbed out, retrieving the sniper rifle from the trunk. My hands were steady as I checked the weapon, but my heart hammered against my ribs.

"Follow the path through the trees," Cristian instructed. "Marco will be waiting for you."

I nodded and started down the trail, the dense foliage swallowing me up. When I emerged into a small clearing, a towering man stepped forward, his presence commanding.

"Beckett." Marco's voice was a low rumble as he extended a hand. "Let's get you set up."

He led me through the underbrush to a spot overlooking the warehouse, where I would have a clear shot of the entire area. "We've got twelve men stationed around the compound. We've counted about twenty armed guards on the premises. About an hour ago, a busload of women arrived. Fourteen were taken inside."

"Fourteen?" I echoed, a cold knot of dread coiling in my stomach. "There were supposed to be fifteen."

"We couldn't get close enough to identify all of them, but one girl was missing. I don't know what that means."

The cold dread in my stomach turned to ice as I took my position, setting up the rifle and adjusting the scope. I couldn't shake the feeling that something was wrong. My gut was screaming at me, warning me that this was going to go sideways.

A flash of headlights cut through the darkness as another SUV pulled up to the warehouse. Through the scope, I saw a man get out, his portly figure unmistakable even at a distance. He yanked a chain leash, and a woman stumbled out behind him, her body barely covered, her hair unnaturally blonde.

My finger tightened on the trigger as rage coiled hot and violent in my chest. I couldn't see her face, but the bruises on her back, the way she moved—it was clear she'd been beaten, broken. My stomach twisted as I watched her struggle to keep up, her movements jerky, like a puppet on strings.

"Looks like the bastard kept one for himself," Marco growled beside me, his voice dripping with disgust. "I hope he dies tonight."

"Yeah," I muttered, my voice tight. "Me too."

As I settled in, the world narrowed to the view through my scope, my breath slow and steady as I waited for the signal. This was it. Everything I was, everything I'd ever done, had led me to this moment.

I prayed for the chance to end Manuel Costa's reign of terror, to put a bullet through his skull and send him straight to hell. But more than that, I prayed to get Carmela out alive.

Because only then could I go back to Celestina and Emilia. Only then could I finally be free.

twenty-one

BECKETT

IT FELT like hours had passed as I lay prone on the hillside, my body rigid, every muscle locked in a tense, vigilant state. My rifle was a comforting weight against my shoulder, the scope framing the warehouse in the crosshairs. My finger hovered over the trigger, poised and ready to strike at the first sign of trouble. But instead of the clean, precise signal I'd been waiting for, the night exploded into chaos.

The initial crack of gunfire was like a slap to the senses, followed almost instantly by a cacophony of screams. The warehouse door burst open, and people surged out in a blind panic, their faces masks of terror and desperation. My heart seized in my chest, adrenaline flooding my veins as I watched the scene unravel in front of me. Women stumbled, their clothes torn and eyes wild, while men shoved past them, clutching wounds, some dragging others who couldn't run on their own.

For a moment, I was frozen, the shock of it all holding me in place. But then instinct kicked in, and I was moving, scrambling to my feet. My rifle swung across my back as I half-

"

slid, half-ran down the steep slope, my boots slipping on the loose dirt and gravel. The cold night air burned in my lungs, every breath a harsh rasp as I raced toward the chaos.

Marco was waiting at the bottom, his eyes wide, his breath coming in sharp bursts. His face, like mine, was smeared with dirt and sweat, his jaw clenched tight against the panic that was threatening to break free.

"What the fuck is happening?" I demanded, my voice raw, almost drowned out by the shouts and screams echoing from the warehouse.

"I don't know," he said, his voice strained. He pressed a finger to his ear, his brow furrowing. "Comms are down. We're blind in there. We have to go inside.

The thought of what could be happening to Carmela—or Sofia, or any of the others—made my blood run cold. I nodded sharply, and we shoved our way through the crowd, pushing against the tide of people still flooding out of the building.

Inside, the scene was a nightmare. The stench of blood and gunpowder filled the air, intermingling with the sickly-sweet scent of fear and sweat. Bodies lay strewn across the concrete floor, some motionless, others writhing in pain, their cries of agony piercing the darkness. The air was thick with smoke, stinging my eyes and choking my lungs as I scanned the room, searching for any sign of the people I cared about.

My gaze locked onto Lorenzo, his face twisted in a mask of rage and desperation. He was standing near the back of the room, his hand gripping the butt of his pistol so tightly that his knuckles shone white in the dim light. I followed his gaze and felt my own stomach twist with anger and disgust.

Gael had a man pinned against the wall. His gun was pressed hard against the bastard's temple. Even from where I stood, I could see the rage in his eyes, the barely restrained violence simmering just below the surface. He was shouting, his words lost in the chaos, but it was clear from his body language that he was demanding answers.

Marco touched my arm, his eyes flicking toward the stage. I followed his gaze and felt a cold, hard knot of rage form in my gut. A man was crouched over a woman, his body shielding her from view, but even from a distance, I could see her trembling, her terror palpable. The sight of her helplessness, the knowledge of what she might have endured, sent a red haze of fury through my vision.

I was moving before I'd even made a conscious decision, my feet pounding against the concrete as I shoved my way through the throng of bodies. My gun was raised, ready to fire, but the crowd was too dense, the risk of hitting an innocent too high.

I was almost at the stage when a piercing scream cut through the din, sharp and high, freezing the blood in my veins. I turned, my heart in my throat, and saw Sofia struggling, her eyes wide and frantic as a fat bastard in a suit dragged her toward a side door, his thick arm wrapped around her throat in a vicious chokehold.

Gael was still grappling with his own opponent, a knife flashing in the dim light as they fought for control. My pulse thundered in my ears, my muscles coiled with the need to act, to help. But before I could take a single step, the man Gael had pinned slumped to the floor, blood pooling around his head.

"Beckett!" Alex's shout came too late as something heavy slammed into me from behind. I hit the ground hard, the impact driving the air from my lungs in a painful whoosh. My rifle clattered away, and I struggled to turn, my fingers scrabbling for the knife at my belt as my attacker tried to pin me down.

The bastard was strong, his weight crushing me into the concrete as he fought to wrestle my arms down. My vision blurred with pain and fury as I twisted beneath him, my elbow driving back into his ribs. He grunted, his grip loosening just enough for me to roll to the side and swing my arm up, the blade of my knife catching the side of his neck.

The man let out a choked cry, his hands flying to his throat as blood spurted between his fingers. I shoved him off, grabbing for my rifle and bringing it up in one smooth motion. His eyes widened in shock and fear as I squeezed the trigger, the bullets slamming into his chest and abdomen in rapid succession.

He jerked with each impact, his body convulsing as blood sprayed out in a gruesome arc. I watched, detached, as he crumpled to the floor, his breath rattling in his chest. My own breath was coming in ragged gasps, the adrenaline pounding through me in a dizzying rush.

Forcing myself to my feet, I scanned the room, my eyes zeroing in on Gael as he sprinted toward the door, Sofia limp in his arms. My heart lurched as I saw the dark bruises marring her throat, the way her head lolled against his shoulder. But she was alive—thank God, she was alive.

Marco was cutting a path through the room, his gun spitting fire as he took down any threat in his path. The brutality of it, the sheer efficiency with which he moved, was both terrifying and awe-inspiring. I turned back to the stage, my heart in my throat, but the man who had been there—Alex, I was almost certain—was gone. The woman he'd been protecting eyes gone too, vanished like ghosts in the chaos.

"Shit!" I swore, the word tearing from my throat like a curse. "We need to clear this place. There could be more women inside. One of them might be Carmela."

Marco nodded. His face turned grim as we pushed deeper into the warehouse. The sounds of violence had faded, replaced by an eerie, oppressive silence that pressed in on all sides. My heart pounded in my ears as we moved through the maze of bodies and debris, the air thick with the coppery tang of blood and the acrid stench of smoke.

We reached a heavy steel door, its surface smeared with bloody handprints. My stomach clenched with a sick sense of foreboding as Marco reached for the handle, his jaw tight.

"You ready?" His voice was low, tense.

I nodded, lifting my gun, my finger hovering over the trigger. "Yeah. If there are guards in there, they're not walking out."

Marco pushed the door open, and my heart dropped into my stomach. The room beyond was a scene from hell. Women lay crumpled on the floor, their bodies twisted and broken, blood pooling around them in dark, sticky puddles.

"What the fuck?" Lorenzo's voice was hoarse with shock and horror.

I forced myself to step inside, my throat tight, my hands shaking. The silence was suffocating, each breath a struggle as I knelt beside the nearest woman. Her eyes were open, staring sightlessly at the ceiling, her skin cold and clammy under my fingers. I reached for her neck, hoping against hope, but there was nothing. No pulse, no sign of life.

"Dead," Marco said quietly, his voice a ghost in the stillness. He moved methodically from one body to the next, his face a mask of grim determination as he checked for signs of life. "They're all dead."

"No." Lorenzo's voice was raw, desperate. He was kneeling beside the last girl, his hands shaking as he pressed his fingers to her neck. "This one's alive. She's alive."

I was at his side in an instant, my heart hammering as I reached out to help lift the girl's limp body. She was barely breathing, her pulse weak and fluttering, but it was there. She was alive.

"We need to get her out of here," I said, my voice tight with urgency.

Marco reached out to take her, but Lorenzo pulled back, cradling her against his chest. "I've got her," he snapped, his eyes blazing with a fierce protectiveness.

Marco hesitated, then nodded. "Let's go. We'll get her some help, then we'll find out where Alex went."

We moved quickly, every step a reminder of the lives we hadn't been able to save. As we made our way back outside, the sound of helicopter blades filled the air, a low, ominous thrum that sent a shiver of dread down my spine.

We rounded the corner just in time to see a chopper lifting off, its rotors kicking up a storm of dust and debris. I raised my rifle, my finger twitching on the trigger, but the bird was already too high. A figure appeared in the open hatch, and I froze, my blood turning to ice.

"Stop the fucking chopper!" I yelled in a voice barely audible over the roar of the blades.

Then, as if in slow motion, a body tumbled from the opening, hitting the ground with a sickening crunch. I was running before I even registered what I was seeing, my heart pounding in my ears as I skidded to a stop beside the crumpled figure.

"Fuck…Alex!" I dropped to my knees, my hands moving frantically over his body. Blood poured from a gaping wound in his abdomen, soaking through his shirt and pooling beneath him. "Goddamn it, man. Hold on."

I tore off my shirt, pressing it against the wound, my hands slick with his blood. He groaned, his eyes fluttering open, the pain in them a mirror of the agony twisting in my chest.

"Carmela," he whispered, his voice a ragged breath.

"Don't move," I begged, my voice breaking. "Just stay with me, okay? We're going to get you out of here."

"Carmela," he repeated, his eyes unfocused as he tried to push himself up. I shoved him back, my hands trembling as I pressed down harder, trying to stem the flow of blood.

"I've got you," I said, my voice thick with desperation. "Just hold on."

His eyes rolled back, his body going limp as he slipped into unconsciousness. I glanced up, my heart twisting as I saw Lorenzo standing over us, his gaze fixed on the helicopter that was now a distant blur on the horizon.

"You think she's on there?" His voice was hollow, filled with a kind of hopelessness that I recognized all too well.

"Yeah," I said, my throat tight. "I do."

The sound of gunfire shattered the stillness, and we turned just in time to see the chopper's tail dip forward, the whole bird spiraling out of control. I watched, helpless, as it crashed into the trees, a massive fireball lighting up the sky.

"Fuck," Lorenzo breathed, the word barely audible over the roar of the flames.

An SUV skidded to a stop beside us, and Marco jumped out, his eyes wide as he took in the scene. "What the hell happened?"

"That was the helicopter that shoved Alex out after shooting him," I said, hoisting Alex's limp body into my arms. "We need to get him to the plane."

Lorenzo scooped up the unconscious woman, her body sagging against him as he climbed into the car. My mind raced as we sped back to the airstrip, the weight of what had happened pressing down on me like a physical force.

We hadn't just failed to bring Carmela home. We'd lost Alex in the process, the man who would have moved heaven and earth to save her. The thought of telling Celestina—of seeing her break under the weight of yet another loss—was almost more than I could bear.

The plane was a flurry of movement as we pulled up, medical personnel rushing to meet us. They lifted Alex onto a makeshift bed

twenty-two

CELESTINA

BECKETT HAD SPENT three agonizing weeks combing through the jungles of Colombia, his heart and hope dwindling with each fruitless day. When he finally returned home, his spirit was broken—he had come back without her. Carmela was still missing, and with each passing second, the guilt and despair ate away at him like a ravenous beast. He'd seen Alex nearly die trying to save her. But even as the man's body slowly healed, the emotional damage of losing her was a wound that would never truly mend.

"You should try to get up." I stood hesitantly in the doorway of Alex's room, my voice barely holding steady. "She wouldn't want you to sit around like this, not when you're lucky to be alive."

"Lucky?" His voice lashed out, jagged and bitter, a blade sharp enough to slice through my heart. "I wish I was dead. She was in my grasp, Celestina. I had her, then…" He stopped, eyes squeezing shut as if that could block out the haunting image. I knew the scene replayed in his head like a twisted, endless loop, the chopper spinning out of control, her hand slipping from his. "I should have gone down with her in that fucking helicopter."

"No," I said firmly, the word hanging in the tense air between us. "You shouldn't have. And you and I both know that she could be alive."

"That's unrealistic," Alex scoffed, his voice raw and frayed. He turned away, his gaze distant, staring through the window as if he could see her somewhere out there, lost but alive. "Even if she is alive, she won't be the same person. I've lost the first woman I've ever really loved."

The admission cut deep, his words stripping away his usual stoic armor. For a moment, the vulnerable man behind the unyielding soldier was laid bare. His eyes, usually hard and guarded, were now awash with pain, glistening with unshed tears.

"And that's my fault." The words were a whisper, carrying the weight of a thousand regrets. "I'll have to live with that knowledge forever. But I'm telling you, she's not dead, Alex. I feel it in my bones." I pressed a hand to my chest, feeling the fierce thrum of hope that had rekindled recently. Before, I'd been trapped in a black void, convinced I'd lost the connection to my twin forever. But now, a light flickered in the darkness—a whisper of her presence I couldn't explain but clung to desperately.

I stepped closer, the need to reach him, to break through his despair, thrumming in my veins. "I thought you were a better man than this. You didn't strike me as a man who'd give up on my sister, Alex. When she comes back, she'll be different, of that I have no doubt. That's when she's going to need your strength. Are you going to just sit there and let your grief pull you under, or are you going to get your ass out of that chair and be the man she's going to need?"

He didn't respond, didn't move. His stillness was a fortress, the walls of his pain too high to scale. I turned away, my heart heavy, and stepped into the hallway. I pulled the door shut behind me with a soft click, the sound echoing like the closing of a chapter. I understood him better than he realized, but until he could see beyond his own grief, beyond the guilt that was drowning him, he was going to have to figure this out on his own. I could only hope that when—**not if**—she came back, he'd be ready.

"I take it he didn't want to hear what you had to say."

Beckett's voice drifted down the hall, a welcome sound on my frayed nerves. My eyes snapped to him, standing there with his strong frame propped against the wall. Before I knew what I was doing, I was running to him, my body colliding with his as I threw myself into his arms. His embrace was solid, grounding me in a way only he could. My legs wrapped around his waist as if anchoring myself to the one constant in my life that still made sense.

"I missed you too, Butterfly," he whispered, his voice a deep rumble against my ear. His fingers wove through my hair, his touch both gentle and possessive, as if he were afraid to let go. He tilted my chin up and his lips found mine, the kiss soft at first, then deepening as a torrent of pent-up emotion surged between us. The relief of having him here, alive, safe, broke something inside me. I sobbed against him, my tears soaking into his shirt as I clung to him.

"Hey, I'm here. Don't cry." His voice cracked as he held me

tighter, his hands trembling. The pain and exhaustion in his eyes mirrored my own.

Pulling back slightly, I cupped his face, forcing him to look at me. "I'm just happy you're here. I couldn't bear losing you too, Beckett. Not now…not when I just got you back."

"I'm not going anywhere, baby." He carried me through the hallway into our room, the door shutting behind us with a finality that sealed us off from the outside world. Here, in this space, it was just us—no pain, no fear, just the two of us and the love that had grown fierce and unyielding through every storm we'd faced.

"Where's Emilia?" I asked, glancing around the room, the emptiness almost unsettling.

"Catarina has her. She knew we needed some time alone. You want me to go get her?" Beckett's hesitation was palpable, as if he was afraid to break the fragile moment we were sharing.

"No. I need you, Beckett." The words came out in a rush, desperate and raw.

He moved to the bed, laying me down gently, his hands trailing up and down my arms, his touch reassuring and reverent. "Marry me, Butterfly."

The world seemed to stop. My heart stuttered, then raced as I stared up at him, my mind struggling to catch up. "What?" The word was barely a whisper, my voice trembling with shock.

"Marry me," he repeated, his gaze intense and unwavering. "Say you'll be mine. Say we can be a family. Say I can love you until the end of time, because if I can't, this life isn't worth living. You're it for me, Butterfly."

Emotion swelled in my chest, so powerful I could barely breathe. Wrapping my arms around his neck, I pulled him down, my lips brushing against his as I whispered, "Yes. I love you, Beckett."

His hands moved with a new urgency, pushing up my shirt, his lips following the path of his hands as he kissed my skin. His touch was fire, igniting every nerve, every cell, until I was a trembling mess beneath him. My own hands found his shirt, yanking it off with a fierceness that matched his own, needing to feel his skin against mine.

Time blurred as we came together, bodies and souls melding in a dance as old as time. The world outside ceased to exist, the pain and loss forgotten in the heat of our passion, in the strength of our love.

Afterward, as we lay tangled together, his breath warm against my hair, I traced the curves of his chest, detecting the steady throb of his heart beneath my palm.

"Were you serious?" I asked softly.

"About what?"

"Marrying me."

Beckett shifted, rolling to face me, his eyes soft but serious. "I'd marry you right now, Celestina. I don't want to go another day without you being mine in every way possible."

"It's crazy that you dond my sister-in-law are cousins." My voice was laced with a disbelief I still hadn't shaken off. Beckett's family history had been a revelation that had turned everything upside down. Madison, who had thought she was alone in the world, now had a family she never knew existed. And Beckett, always the loner, had found something he didn't even know he was missing.

"It's weird for me, too," he admitted, his voice thick with regret. "I hate that I was here and could have helped her. Instead, she fought to survive in this world alone. It gutted me to know she'd been in foster care. I could have taken her in."

I pressed a kiss to his chest, feeling his pain like a shadow in my own heart. "You couldn't have done anything, Beckett. You aren't that much older than she is… Besides, you were in the Marines while she was in foster care."

"Maybe she could have been the reason I came home. Maybe then I wouldn't have gone to jail like my father."

"Then we wouldn't have met." I pushed up onto my elbow, needing him to see the truth in my eyes. "I'd give anything to have my sister back, but I wouldn't change a damn thing. This mess gave me you and Emilia."

His arms tightened around me, his hold fierce and protective. "Let's go get married."

"Okay."

His eyes widened, surprise flickering across his features. "Are you serious?"

"Yes. I need something happy right now, and being your wife would make me the happiest."

Beckett's face lit up with a joy so pure it took my breath away. He scrambled out of bed, gathering me in his arms as if afraid I'd change my mind.

"What are you doing?" I laughed as he lifted me effortlessly, his excitement infectious.

"Taking you to the shower before you change your mind. By tonight…you'll be mine forever."

As we moved, my heart swelled with a fierce, unyielding love. No matter what lay ahead, no matter the darkness we would still have to face, I knew this: we would face it together, as a family. And that hope, that love, was stronger than any fear.

epilogue

ALEX

I WANTED to hate her for existing. I wanted to despise the way the room lit up when Celestina and Beckett announced the gender of their babies, how everyone beamed and laughed, their joy spilling over like a glass of champagne filled to the brim. I wanted to, but I couldn't. It wasn't her fault that Carmela was still missing—it was mine.

I could still feel her in my grasp, the delicate bones of her wrist under my fingers, the frantic pulse that matched my own as we dangled over the abyss. And then I was falling, the roar of the wind swallowing my screams as her hand slipped from mine. The look of pure terror in her eyes, wide and dark, was seared into my mind, an endless, tormenting loop that haunted every moment of rest. I closed my eyes and there she was, slipping through my fingers all over again. Four months had passed, and I was no closer to finding the woman I loved.

Celestina clung to hope like a drowning woman to a lifeline, her belief that Carmela was alive burning bright even as I watched it slowly flicker and fade with each passing day. Hell, I was starting to doubt my own gut, the one thing I'd always trusted. How could I believe in anything when every lead, every desperate chase, ended in nothing?

"How are you holding up?" Massimo's voice was a gentle intrusion into the storm of my thoughts. He settled beside me on the porch, his presence solid and familiar, offering a cold beer with a small, tentative smile. "I'm worried about you, Alex."

"I'm fine." The lie tasted bitter, coating my tongue like ash. Massimo knew better. We'd been through too much, seen too much, for me to bullshit him now. If it hadn't been for him, I'd be rotting in a Colombian jail cell, broken and useless.

He didn't say anything, just raised one dark eyebrow in that way of his, calling me out without a word. "You might convince yourself of that bullshit, but I know differently. You're barely existing, my friend."

"How am I supposed to exist without her?" I snapped, my voice harsh and brittle. My gaze drifted to where Madison sat, her hand resting on the swell of her stomach, her face glowing with a kind of peace I'd never seen before. "Could you survive without Madison?"

His eyes softened, following mine to his wife, his world. "No."

"Then why would you expect me to do it? I'm in love with your sister, Massimo, only she was taken before we had a chance together. And then I lost her in Colombia. She was right there, in my fucking hands, and I lost her."

"Bullshit." Massimo's voice was a sharp, cutting blade. He set his drink down with a force that made the glass rattle on the table. "That motherfucker Manuel is to blame for everything that's happened. He fucked with Catarina, then Celestina. Had it not been for Beckett falling for her, who knows if she'd be here now? What happened to Carmela is no one's fault but that monster who took her. And we will get her back, Alex. I won't stop until she comes home—dead or alive."

"You think she's dead?" My voice broke, the question hanging in the air like a noose, tightening around my throat.

"No, I don't."

"Then how are you holding onto that hope, Massimo? I want to believe it—" I shook my head, the motion feeling futile "But it's been four months."

He sighed, his gaze darkening with the weight of his own pain and loss. "Matias learned that several men running an auction were slaughtered the night before the event. The women rescued swore it was a woman who'd set them free."

"A woman?" I frowned, confusion muddling the grim picture in my head.

"Yes, a woman. The women who were saved called her the *Angelo Della Misericordia*."

His words caused me straighten in my chair. "Angel of Mercy. And you think…"

He nodded, his expression grim and hopeful all at once. "Yes. I think Carmela is alive… and I think she may have a little more Vincenzo in her than we realize." He stood, tossing his empty bottle into the trash with a force that betrayed his simmering anger. "You need to prepare yourself, Alex. When, not if, we find Carmela, she might not be the woman you remember."

"I don't care. I just want her back." The words were a growl, torn from the depths of my soul. I didn't care if she was scarred, if she was broken. I just needed her here, in my arms, where she belonged.

"We all do." His hand was a comforting weight on my shoulder, his grip strong and steady. "We'll find her, Alex."

I nodded, unable to trust my voice. I watched as he moved across the room toward Celestina and Madison, his back straight, his shoulders squared with the kind of determination that could move mountains. My body was finally, mostly healed from the injuries I'd sustained when I'd been shot and shoved out of that helicopter, but the pain that lingered was a shadow compared to the agony of losing her.

Pushing to my feet, I waved absently toward the others and headed inside the house. Massimo had spent a fortune buying up the land around Michael's house, building a fortress for the people he loved. For the last five months, crews had worked tirelessly, erecting homes for the family on the sprawling acreage. Each structure was a testament to his love and fear—a way to protect those he couldn't bear to lose again. One of the houses was mine...and when Carmela finally came home, it would be hers too.

The thought was a lifeline, something to cling to in the dark hours of the night when doubt and despair threatened to drag me under.

Shoving through the massive kitchen, I headed up to my room and locked the door behind me. The silence was heavy, suffocating, but it was better than the constant, buzzing chaos outside. Massimo thought he was telling me something new, some sliver of hope I hadn't already grasped for, but he was wrong. I'd spent countless hours scouring every scrap of information on Carmela, piecing together the stories of the *Angelo Della Misericordia*.

It wasn't hard to connect the dots, to see the truth lurking beneath the rumors and whispers. The only thing I couldn't wrap my mind around was the description of the woman the survivors had seen. It didn't match Carmela, not in any way I remembered. But then again, what had she gone through in these months of captivity? How had the ordeal twisted her, changed her?

I sat on the edge of the bed, the weight of everything squeezing me like a vise. She was out there, somewhere, fighting, surviving. My Carmela. My warrior. I could almost feel her presence, a ghost brushing against the edges of my consciousness.

I'd find her. I'd bring her back, no matter what it took. And when I did, I would never let her go.

For now, all I could do was wait, to gather my strength, to prepare for the day I could hold her again. And when that day came, nothing in this world or the next would take her from me again.

bonus epilogue
MADISON

FUCK.

The two pink lines stared up at me, taunting me from the palm of my hand. How the hell had I let this happen? Sure, in this family, pregnancies spread like the flu, but I'd managed to dodge it for years—until now.

A sharp pang of anxiety twisted in my chest as I looked around the small, cramped bathroom, feeling suddenly trapped by the tiled walls and my own reality. The timing couldn't have been worse. The chaos around us had taken over every waking minute of our lives—well, almost every minute, judging by the unexpected test result I was clutching. Celestina had nearly died and had just come home from the hospital after giving birth to my newest niece, Emilia. This was the absolute worst possible time for another surprise baby.

"Madison?" Massimo's voice boomed through the hallway, snapping me out of my daze as he pushed open the bathroom door, his eyes wide with concern. "Are you okay? Freddy said he took you to the drugstore because you weren't feeling well." He stepped into the bathroom, his gaze dropping to the white stick I held between my trembling fingers. "Madison?" His eyes traveled up my body, finally locking onto mine, filled with a mix of confusion and concern.

I swallowed hard, trying to mask the storm of emotions swirling inside me. Forcing a smile, I managed a weak, "Surprise?"

He blinked, his brow furrowing as he tried to make sense of what he was seeing. "Surprise?" His confusion deepened, the crease between his eyebrows growing more pronounced. "I don't understand. What is that?"

A nervous laugh bubbled out of me, sounding strange and hollow even to my own ears. I thrust the test toward him, watching as realization slowly dawned on his face.

"We're pregnant."

"Pregnant." He whispered the word like it was something fragile, something he was afraid would shatter if he spoke too loudly. His fingers brushed over the plastic stick, his gaze lifting to meet mine, eyes shimmering with unshed tears. "You're pregnant?" His voice was barely a whisper now, filled with awe. "We're having a baby?"

"Yeah." I nodded, biting down on my lip to keep it from trembling. "It appears so." The silence stretched between us, my heart racing as I searched his face for any hint of disappointment or anger. "I'm sorry. I guess I forgot to get my shot with everything that's been happening with Celestina. I know we aren't married yet, but—"

He pulled me into his arms, cutting off my rambling apologies, his embrace warm and strong, the steady beat of his heart a reassuring rhythm against my ear. He buried his face in my neck, his breath hot on my skin as he whispered, his voice thick with emotion, "I love you."

I leaned back, searching his face, my own eyes filling with tears now. "You're not mad? I mean…we had everything planned. The wedding in Italy, plus everything that's going on."

"I don't care about the damn wedding, Madison." His voice was fierce, the conviction in his eyes leaving no room for doubt. "I mean…yes, I want to be married to you, but the big white dress and church aren't important to me." He pressed a tender kiss to my forehead, pulling me even tighter against him. "You are important to me."

"I know…but I promised Celestina she could focus on the wedding." My voice wavered, the guilt of stealing even a moment of happiness weighing on me.

"She still can," he assured me gently, his hands cradling my face. "But we'll already be married." He tossed the pregnancy test onto the dresser and turned back to me, his eyes darkening with an intensity that made my knees weak. "But not until I show you just how happy this makes me."

With a swift, possessive motion, he grabbed my hips and pulled me flush against his chest. His lips descended on mine, the kiss full of passion, pouring every ounce of his love and happiness into it. Massimo had owned me from the moment he swept me into his arms the night my apartment was broken into all those years ago. And now, as he guided me toward the bed, the world seemed to narrow to just us—

two hearts, two bodies, and the new life growing between us.

Gripping the hem of my sundress, he yanked it over my head, his eyes burning with a fierce hunger as he took in my bare skin. "Sexy as fuck," he growled, his palm flattening against my belly. "I can't wait until this belly is swollen with my child. Madison, you've given me everything I never knew I deserved."

His fingers deftly unclasped my bra, the cool air grazing my heated skin as he slid the fabric down my arms. My nipples pebbled under his gaze, a low, appreciative growl rumbling in his chest. He shoved my panties down, his eyes never leaving mine, his touch reverent and possessive.

"This pussy is mine," he murmured, his voice a husky command that sent a shiver of anticipation racing down my spine.

My cry of pleasure echoed through the room as he buried his face between my thighs, his tongue delving between my folds with the skill of a man who knew exactly how to unravel me. Each swipe of his tongue, each flick of his finger, sent shockwaves through my body, my insides clenching around the pleasure he so expertly coaxed from me. When he slid a finger inside, my orgasm crashed over me like a tidal wave, my walls pulsing and tightening around him.

"Fuck, you're beautiful when you come." Massimo's voice was thick with arousal as he pulled his finger free, bringing it to his lips and licking it clean, his gaze never leaving mine.

I watched through half-lidded eyes as he stripped off his clothes, the raw power of his body making my pulse race. His cock stood thick and proud, his hand wrapping around it as he moved toward me, a predatory gleam in his eyes. When he climbed between my legs and pushed inside me, it felt like coming home. We moved together, bodies and souls melded in a dance as old as time, each thrust taking me higher, closer to the edge of ecstasy.

Our moans and gasps filled the room, our bodies straining and clinging, his name a broken prayer on my lips as I soared, crashing over the edge, pulling him with me. Massimo's growl of release vibrated through my entire being as his seed filled me, marking me, claiming me in a way that made my heart ache with love and need.

When he finally stilled, his body draped over mine, he rolled to the side, pulling me into his arms, his breath hot and ragged against my hair. "I love you, Bella. Even in the darkest of times, you've made me the happiest I've ever been." His voice was soft, a promise and a prayer all in one. He pressed a gentle kiss to my lips before sitting up, his expression serious.

"But now we need to get married."

"Massimo." I groaned, flopping back onto the bed, my heart still racing from the intensity of what we'd just shared. "You seriously want to go get married? How the hell will we pull that off?"

He grinned, the mischievous sparkle in his eyes making my heart flutter. "Easy… Elvis."

I stared at him, caught between laughter and exasperation. "Elvis? As in a Vegas wedding?"

"Yes, a Vegas wedding." He grinned wider, the boyish excitement on his face impossible to resist. "We'll fly out tonight. We'll make it official. You, me, and our baby."

Tears welled in my eyes, happy tears this time, as I reached up, cupping his face in my hands. "You're crazy, you know that?"

"I'm crazy about you, Bella." His voice was tender, his eyes shining with a love that left me breathless. "And I'm not waiting another minute to make you mine."

As he leaned down to kiss me, I knew that no matter what lay ahead, we would face it together—married, in love, and ready to take on the world, one crazy, wonderful step at a time.

___

She thought I was kidding when I said we were going to get married. I wasn't. As soon as we cleaned up from our mid-afternoon tryst, I made sure Drew and Donny knew we were heading out—without them. Madison's only condition was that we keep it hidden until the storm surrounding Celestina and Carmela blew over. I agreed, though deep down, I knew that storm was far from passing, especially when Carmela's where-abouts were still a mystery. But I couldn't wait. There was no way I was bringing my child into this world without putting my ring on Madison's finger. My grandmother would have my hide if I let her go through this pregnancy without my last name.

Despite what Madison believed, my *Nonna* would prefer this over having her great-grandchild born out of wedlock. The thought of facing her wrath made me nervous, but the idea of Madison hesitating, of maybe not wanting this as much as I did, was a thousand times worse.

"Hey, hey there, big fella. You look like your nerves are getting the better of you. Just take a deep breath for me… Your lady will be poppin' on out here in two shakes." The Elvis impersonator, with his exaggerated sideburns and slicked-back hair, patted me on the shoulder, his voice a soft drawl as he gave me an encouraging smile.

I nodded, barely hearing him over the roar of my own heartbeat. "I hope so." I blew out a deep breath, trying to will the nerves to stop racing inside me. "Did she say—"

The words died on my lips the moment Madison stepped out from behind the closed door. A surge of emotion made my breath catch in my throat, my chest tightening as I took her in. She was wearing a white silk gown that hugged her curves like a second skin, the fabric shimmering in the soft chapel lights. Her hair was pinned to the side, a cascade of dark waves tumbling over her bare shoulder. My entire body buzzed with a need so fierce, I felt like I might spontaneously combust.

"Take a breath, my man. Don't want you passing out before she makes it to the end," the fake Elvis whispered, but his words barely registered.

She was breathtaking. My Madison, looking like an angel, her beauty glowing from the inside out. The soft melody of "Can't Help Falling in Love" filled the small chapel, but I barely heard it. The world narrowed to just her, moving toward me with that shy, radiant smile, her eyes never leaving mine.

When she reached me, she took my hands, her fingers cool and soft against my trembling ones. I squeezed them gently, grounding myself in her touch, in the reality that this extraordinary woman was about to become my wife.

"Dearly beloved…"

I never thought I'd hear wedding vows sung like a rock ballad, but then again, I'd never imagined I'd be getting married in a Vegas chapel by an Elvis impersonator. The surrealness of it all made me smile, but it was her, the woman I'd fallen hopelessly in love with, who held my attention. Her thumb brushed over the top of my hand, a small, grounding caress that sent warmth spreading through me.

"What?" I glanced at the officiant, startled out of my thoughts.

"You gonna speak your vows?" Elvis asked, his tone light and teasing, but his eyes kind and understanding.

Nodding, I tightened my hold on her hands, drawing strength from the way she looked at me—like I was her whole world.

"Madison…" My voice caught, and I swallowed hard, the emotions thick in my throat. "When you walked into my office that night…it was as if my world stopped moving. My past, present, and future collided in a single moment. Without a doubt, I knew you would be mine. When I nearly fucked it all up and pushed you away, my heart stopped beating. Without you, I'm half the man I should be. You complete me in ways I never knew I needed or wanted. The world may think I'm in charge, but the truth is, you are. You have my heart, my protection, and my unwavering loyalty. Without you, life means nothing."

Tears spilled over her lashes, but they weren't tears of

sadness. They were tears of joy, of relief, of a love so deep it was almost tangible between us.

"Wow. I'm not sure I can follow that," she whispered, a laugh breaking through her tears as she slipped the golden band onto my finger. She took a deep breath, her eyes never leaving mine. "When I lost my mother, and then my father, I thought I'd never feel that kind of love again. And I was right…because what I feel for you is something infinitely better. You show me every day what being loved and cared for feels like. I was certain I'd be alone for a long time, but you knocked me off my feet and barreled through the iron gate I had around my heart. I can't imagine life without you, nor do I want to. I knew being with you came with risk, but I also know you'll do everything to ensure I'm safe and, above all else, loved. I waited my whole life for a man like you, Massimo. No, that's not right. I waited for a family like the one you gave me and are giving me. I love you yesterday, today, and tomorrow."

"Well…You can kiss your bride."

The music swelled around us, but all I could see, all I could feel, was the woman in my arms, the one who'd turned my world upside down and made it better than I'd ever dreamed possible. I cupped her face, brushing a stray tear from her cheek with my thumb, and then I kissed her, slow and deep, pouring every ounce of love and gratitude I had into that single moment.

Taking over as the head of my family's empire was something I'd prepared myself for from the time I understood what being an Anastasi meant. But nothing had prepared me for this—for the fierce, all-consuming love I felt for this woman, my wife, the mother of my child.

"How about we go celebrate being married?" I murmured against her lips, the words a soft, teasing promise.

"Every day is a celebration with you, Massimo." She smiled up at me, her eyes shining with a love that made my heart ache in the best possible way. "So, why don't you just take me home and make love to me as your wife for the first time?"

"You're pretty damn smart, Bella." I scooped her up into my arms, her laughter ringing out as I carried her down the aisle, past the grinning Elvis, past the empty rows of seats, and out into the warm Vegas night. "Let's go home, Mrs. Anastasi."

"Let's, Mr. Anastasi."

And as I carried her out of the chapel, the stars above us bright and sparkling, I knew one thing for certain: life with her, with our child, was going to be the most incredible journey I'd ever take. And I was ready for every single step.

DON'T WORRY…

Massimo and Madison may have wed in secret.

But they made a promise to hold a grand wedding for Vittoria Anastasi.

And an Anastasi always keeps their promise…even if they aren't the ones getting married.

Mafia Vows: An Anastasi Wedding Short Story Coming in 2025

playlist

Tear Myself Apart *(Tate McRaea)*

Only Love Can Hurt Like This *(Paloma Faith)*

My Own Prison *(Creed)*

Who Am I *(Needtobreathe, Elle King)*

Sorry *(Buckcherry)*

Chaotic *(Tate McRae)*

Stay *(Rhianna)*

Sex On Fire *(Kings of Leon)*

Love Again *(Dua Lipa)*

Vicious *(Tate McRae)*

The Monster *(Eminem)*

I Don't Care *(Apocalyptica)*

The Scientist *(Coldplay)*

Never Say Never *(The Fray)*

Hurt *(Christina Aguilera)*

Savage Hearts Playlist on Spotify

about dori

"Love, Loyalty, and the Occasional Gunshot."

Dori Pulitano, a USA Today Bestselling Author, is the naughtier, much dirtier half Author LC Taylor. Writing men in shades of grey, the bad girl Dori embraces her Italian side with heroic hitmen, decadent conflicted dons, and oh-so-f*ckable assassins trying to trade their devilish ways for salvation—and the perfect woman to tie to their bed.

And F**k following the rules... this author is most definitely trigger-happy.

www.AlphaBookBoyfriends.com

facebook.com/AlphaBookBoyfriend

tiktok.com/@alphabookboyfriend

instagram.com/alphabookboyfriends

bookbub.com/authors/dori-pulitano

x.com/AlphaBookBoyFrn

www.ingramcontent.com/pod-product-compliance
Lightning Source LLC
Chambersburg PA
CBHW060315310726
48976CB00007B/2337